THE OLD DRAGON OF THE MOUNTAIN'S CHRISTMAS

DRAGON LORDS OF VALDIER BOOK 9

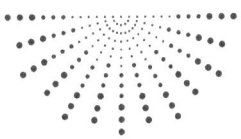

S.E. SMITH

ACKNOWLEDGMENTS

I would like to thank my husband Steve for believing in me and being proud enough of me to give me the courage to follow my dream. I would also like to give a special thank you to my sister and best friend, Linda, who not only encouraged me to write, but who also read the manuscript. Also to my other friends who believe in me: Julie, Jackie, Lisa, Sally, Elizabeth (Beth) and Narelle. The girls that keep me going!

And a special thanks to Paul Heitsch, David Brenin, Samantha Cook, Suzanne Elise Freeman, and PJ Ochlan—the awesome voices behind my audiobooks!

—S. E. Smith

To Dulcie and Jose – for showing that love has no age limits.

The Old Dragon of the Mountain's Christmas: Dragon Lords of Valdier
Book 9

Summary: An alien goddess gives a deformed dragon shifter a second
chance to find love with a human woman on Earth who teaches him
that love can happen at any age.

ISBN: 978-1-942562-82-5 (kdp Paperback)
ISBN: 9781078745550 (BN Paperback)
ISBN: 978-1-942562-81-8 (ebook)

Romance (love, explicit sexual content, older couple) | Fantasy | Para-
normal – Shifters, Magic | Holiday | Science Fiction (Aliens)

Published by Montana Publishing, LLC
& SE Smith of Florida Inc. www.sesmithfl.com

CONTENTS

CAST OF CHARACTERS

For those who have not read the Dragon Lords of Valdier, here is a little background.

The Valdier are dragon shifters. Only the Valdier and their mates can bond with the mysterious and powerful golden symbiots, who are, yes, symbiotic creatures, and they are stand-out characters all on their own! Each Valdier consists of three parts: the dragon, the man/woman, and their symbiot companion. They are friends with the Curizan (a species able to harness the energy around them) and the Sarafin (a cat shifting species). The following is a character guide for those new to the series:

Zoran Reykill, Leader of the Valdier,

true mate to Abby Tanner:

one son: Zohar

Zoran's symbiot: Goldie

Mandra Reykill

true mate to Ariel Hamm:

one son: Jabir

Mandra's symbiot: Precious

Kelan Reykill

true mate to Trisha Grove:

one son: Bálint

Kelan's symbiot: Bio

Trelon Reykill

true mate to Cara Truman:

twin daughters: Amber and Jade

Trelon's symbiot: Symba

Creon Reykill

true mate to Carmen Walker:

twin daughters: Spring and Phoenix

Creon's symbiot: Harvey

Phoenix's symbiot: Stardust

Spring's symbiot: Little Bit

Paul Grove

true mate to Morian Reykill

Cree and Calo Aryeh

true mate to Melina Franklin:

one daughter: Hope

Vox d'Rojah, King of the Sarafin,

mated to Riley St. Claire:

one son: Roam

Viper d'Rojah **mated to** Tina St. Claire

Asim **mated to** Pearl St. Claire

Ha'ven Ha'darra,

Prince of the Curizan,

mated to Emma Watson:

one daughter: Alice

Aikaterina: Unknown species; accepted as a Goddess to the Valdier, she is the oldest and most powerful of her kind.

Arilla and Arosa: Unknown species, still young for their kind, they are twins and thought to be Goddesses.

I hope you enjoy Christoff and Edna's story. I didn't plan to write it, it just came. I knew once I started, I had to finish it. I think I have laughed and cried more through this story than I have any of my others. They were good tears. If you are like me, you'll need a box of tissues for this one!

SYNOPSIS

Born prematurely, Christoff wasn't as big or as strong as his older brother or the other younglings in the village. Unable to fit in, he does the best he can, helping his father and mother on their farm. His life changes when the mountain near their farm awakens. Believing he is the only one who can quiet it, he retreats to the mountain to watch over the village that shunned him.

A hermit for centuries, he dreams of the day he can move on to his next life; a life that he hopes will give him a chance of finding his true mate. He knows his time has come when the mountain begins to tremble again. What he doesn't expect is a group of younglings who suddenly appear in the hopes of saving a thing called Christmas. When the mountain erupts, he never expects to awaken on a strange planet light years away, or to meet an unusual woman who sees beneath his deformity to the warrior hidden within.

Can the love of a special woman and her family heal Christoff's tortured soul? Find out what happens when the Goddess Aikaterina gives The Old Dragon his very own special Christmas.

PROLOGUE

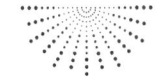

*S*everal centuries before:

Christoff ignored the other young boys and girls in the village as he hurried through it. Several of them stopped, pointed, and laughed at him. He was almost half their size, even though he was the same age. He had been born early and never quite caught up with the others.

"Lemar, wait!" Christoff called out to his older brother.

Lemar grimaced as he glanced over his shoulder at Christoff. "Go home!" he ordered.

"But, father told me to help you bring home the items he needs to fix the irrigation system," Christoff said.

Lemar stopped and angrily turned on his heel to face Christoff. Christoff was used to his older brother being angry at him. It still bothered him, but he tried not to show it. If he did, Lemar would only be meaner to him.

"Go home, Christoff," Lemar replied cruelly. "I don't want to be seen with you."

"But," Christoff started to argue.

He swallowed when Lemar shoved him backwards hard enough to make him fall down. Looking up at his older brother, he tried not to show him how much it hurt. In the background, he heard more snickering and name calling from the other younglings in the village.

"I said go home," Lemar snapped. "You are making a laughing stock out of yourself. I don't want the others thinking I am like you – weak, unfit to be a warrior."

"I'm not weak," Christoff protested. "I help around the farm while you chase the females."

Christoff winced when he saw the rage flash through Lemar's eyes. His dragon and symbiot sensed that his brother was about to lose control again. Christoff released his dragon when he saw his brother shifting. His symbiot formed a thin layer of armor around him. It, like him and his dragon, was smaller and weaker than most of the other young boys.

He rolled to his feet seconds before Lemar struck out at him. The blow hurt as it caught him across the chest, knocking the wind out of him. He knew there would be no way to defeat his brother. The only thing he could do was try to protect himself as much as possible from the beating he was about to receive.

Lemar! Father told me to come help. Please, do not be angry, he murmured as he tried to calm his brother when he struck him again, this time across his left arm.

You never listen! You are weak and useless, Christoff! You shouldn't even be alive, Lemar growled as he struck Christoff again with his tail, leaving a long line of welts across Christoff's back.

I do listen, Christoff defended. *I listen to mother and father. They don't think I am weak and useless.*

Christoff winced as Lemar swung out with his tail and caught him across the jaw. The force of the blow spun him around. A hoarse cry escaped him when Lemar grabbed one of his deformed wings with his sharp teeth and bit down.

His dragon reacted, wrapping his tail around Lemar's left ankle and pulling on it at the same time as he threw himself backwards to ease the pain. The combination knocked both dragons off their feet. Christoff immediately rolled when he felt Lemar release his wing in an effort to protect his back. Tears streamed down his cheeks as he struggled to break free and shakily stood up.

He twisted in fear when Lemar grabbed his leg and kicked out at his brother. A howl of pain escaped him when Lemar sank his sharp claws into his calf. Christoff felt a wave of panic when his leg buckled under him, causing him to fall to the ground again.

Lemar took advantage of his weakness to roll on top of him. The sharp claws that had been in his calf a moment ago, now dug into his throat, cutting off his air supply. He struggled weakly to push Lemar off, but it was no use. His brother outweighed him by almost three to one.

Christoff felt certain that Lemar wasn't going to stop this time. His older brother was embarrassed by him, he knew that, but he never expected him to take his frustration and embarrassment so far as to kill him. Struggling to draw in a breath of air, he gazed up at hatred burning in Lemar's eyes.

No, this time his brother would not stop, Christoff thought in resignation as black spots began to darken his vision. Perhaps, Lemar was right. Perhaps, it would have been better if he had died as an infant.

"Lemar, stop!" one of the elder warriors ordered. "Release your brother now."

Christoff didn't think Lemar would have followed the elder's command if it wasn't for the fact the man's symbiot was snarling at him. Lemar glared down at him one last time before he released him and jerked away, shifting back to his two-legged form as he stepped back from Christoff's limp form.

"He shouldn't be alive," Lemar growled angrily, waving his hand. "He's weak, pathetic! He cannot protect our village and he'll never be good enough to find a mate."

"I know, but it is not your place to kill him," the elder stated. "It is your father's place."

Christoff shifted and rolled until he was sitting up. He wiped at the tears on his cheeks in frustration. He knew Lemar hated him even more when he cried.

"I help father," Christoff defended, rubbing his nose against his arm. "I work hard."

The elder turned to look down at Christoff in disgust. "You will never be fit to be a warrior, youngling. You think you help your parents, but they give you chores not even fit for a female."

Christoff wiped at his face again as more tears escaped when the crowd of villagers chuckled and nodded their heads in agreement. He rose unsteadily to his feet. Clenching his fists at his side, he lifted his head. His father and mother knew that he was not weak. Every day they told him how much he was a gift to them. He worked hard out in the fields beside them while Lemar came to the village to wrestle with the other boys and flirt with the females. He was growing stronger each day. Yes, his wings may never let him fly, but he could still turn into a dragon and fight. His father was teaching him how to and one day, he would beat Lemar and show his older brother that he could defend the village if necessary.

"That is not true," Christoff whispered, staring at the Elder with his head held high. "The bread you eat comes from our fields. I work beside my father and mother to plant, care for, and harvest it. I am not weak!"

The male's eyes narrowed in warning. "Watch your tone with me, boy, or I will finish what your brother started," the elder snarled. "Get what you came for and return home. I will talk with your father about the disruptions that happened today."

Christoff wanted to protest, but both his dragon and his symbiot pressed on him to remain quiet. Turning clumsily on his heel, he ignored the laughter as he made his way to the iron shop. He would get the parts his father needed and return home. He knew that Lemar would not be back until after dark.

"You should have killed him, Lemar," one of the young girls said just loud enough for him to hear. "You are so strong. I can't believe you have a brother like Christoff."

Christoff ignored the wave of pain at the hurtful words. He would show everyone that he was strong and when he did, the Goddess would look down on him and make him, his dragon, and his symbiot whole.

Two months later:

Christoff wiped the sweat from his brow and smiled at his mother. She was carrying a bucket of water for him and his dad. She stumbled under the heavy weight when the ground trembled. Dropping the hoe he was using to clear some of the weeds, he rushed over to help her.

"Here, let me," he said, gently taking the bucket from her.

"Where's Lemar?" she asked, looking around with a frown. "He was supposed to be helping you."

Christoff shrugged his shoulders. Since that day in the village, he had avoided Lemar as much as possible. It wasn't that difficult. His brother seldom did anything around the farm anymore. Lemar preferred to spend his time in the village.

"The mountain is rumbling more than usual," he said instead before bending to pick up the ladle and scooping up some water.

"Christoff," his father called over, staring up at the mountain. "Get the tools and head back to the house. My dragon is warning me that we must leave."

"But, the crops are almost ready," Christoff protested, looking at the field of golden grain. "Surely it will stop again."

Christoff watched as his father hurried down the row toward them. There was a look of determination and… fear in his father's eyes. The determination he had seen before, but the fear – that was new. He had never seen his father afraid of anything. His father wrapped his arm around his mother's waist and began pulling her toward the house.

"Come, we must go to the village," Tallon said in an urgent voice.

"Christoff," his mother called, looking over her shoulder.

"I'm coming, Mother," Christoff said, grabbing the bucket and dumping the water out on the ground. He turned and started following them before he released a curse. He had forgotten the hoe. "Go! I'll be right there."

Christoff turned and hurried back to grab the hoe he had dropped. He stumbled and fell to one knee when the ground shook violently under his feet. Scrambling, he looked up at the mountain that bordered the northwest corner of the valley. A steady stream of smoke was pouring from the top of it and a light rain of ash began drifting down over the valley, covering it in a gray-colored film.

Swallowing down his fear, he turned and hurried back through the field. He fell several more times before he cleared the edge leading down to the house. His symbiot appeared out of the field, looking wildly around for him.

Mountain angry, his dragon hissed. *Smell danger.*

I know, Christoff said, glancing over his shoulder when he heard a low rumble. *Father feels it as well.*

Christoff was almost to the house when a loud explosion shook the valley. The force of the blast sent him sprawling on the ground. He glanced up to see a huge rock, the size of a full grown warrior, falling through the air before it disappeared through the roof of his home. Christoff blinked, watching as his older brother staggered out of the burning house.

"Father! Mother!" Christoff yelled, trying to stand. "Father!" he cried again in fear and confusion.

"Christoff!" Tallon called out from near the barn.

He turned to see his father slowly rising to his feet with his mother's help. Blood ran down one side of his face and he had a long, thin piece of wood embedded in his left thigh. Christoff's dazed gaze moved from a destroyed section of the barn back to his father.

"Your symbiot," Christoff whispered. "Where is it?"

"I sent it to the village this morning with a load of grain," Tallon muttered in pain. "It is coming."

"Father! Mother! We have to leave," Lemar shouted, raising a hand to his head and shaking it as he staggered toward them.

All around them, small and mid-size rocks fell, littering the ground like raindrops. Christoff winced when several larger pieces hit him on the head. He raised his hand to touch a spot near his temple, surprised when he felt a warm dampness.

"Christoff, you're bleeding," his mother cried in dismay, staggering under the weight of her mate.

"Mother, we have to go," Lemar said in a harsh voice, reaching out to grab her arm when she stepped toward Christoff.

"We have to help him," Tallon grimaced, glancing at his oldest son. "You and I can carry him together."

"Leave him," Lemar demanded, glancing at Christoff with anger. "If he cannot fly, let him run."

"Lemar," their mother whispered in distress. "You know Christoff cannot fly. Help your father carry him. I will follow with his symbiot."

"No! He shouldn't have lived! Let the Goddess take him. He is weak," Lemar argued as his symbiot created a cover for him when the hot ash began to ignite small fires. "You have always protected him. Now it is time to protect yourself. Come with me."

"No!" Tasmay cried, pulling her arm away. "You have always treated Christoff as if he was unworthy, when in truth, it is *you* that is unworthy. No warrior would leave someone who is weaker behind," she whispered as a line of dirty tears coursed down her cheeks. "We need your help, Lemar. Please."

Lemar's face twisted as Tallon turned to stare at him. Christoff was about to tell his parents that Lemar was right, that maybe this was the Goddess' way of telling him that he shouldn't have lived when another explosion, this one larger than before, knocked them all to the ground. Christoff's face reflected his fear when he saw the ground opening across the valley and heading toward them.

"Fly!" Lemar shouted in terror as he shifted.

"Lemar!" Tallon roared in pain, turning as his oldest son rose into the ash-filled sky. "Lemar!"

"Father," Christoff said in a quiet voice filled with resignation. "Go. Take mother and go. Lemar and the others are right. If I cannot survive on my own, it is the Goddess' way of showing that I am too weak."

Tallon turned to look at his youngest son's face. He saw the acceptance that he would not make it. Refusing to believe that any boy with so much heart was not also a powerful warrior, he shifted despite the shaft of wood in his upper thigh.

Christoff turned to watch as his father lifted off the ground. A moment later, his mother shifted and lifted off the ground as well. He raised his hand in farewell, only to gasp when his father's dragon reached down and wrapped one clawed foot around his wrists.

"Father, no!" Christoff protested, lifting his other hand up to try to break free. He gasped when his mother grabbed his other wrist in her claw. "Mother! I'm too heavy, especially with father's injury. Leave me and take care of him."

Christoff tried to stop them, but they refused. He felt his feet leave the ground. He ran as best he could under them as they pumped frantically on their wings.

"Leave me, please," Christoff cried as he saw the small holes that began appearing on the wings of his parent's dragons. As fast as their symbiots tried to heal them, more would appear. "Please!"

He cried out when a large piece of flaming debris fell from the sky, shattering one of his mother's wings. He watched in horror as she tumbled to the ground. His father, unable to carry his weight alone with his injuries, was forced to release him as he struggled to reach his injured mate.

Christoff hit the ground hard and rolled. Glancing up, he scrambled to his feet when he saw his father land next to his mother. He was almost to them when the ground shook again. His father looked up at him, staring in regret as he held his mate in his arms.

"I love you, son," Tallon said brokenly, gathering his mate's limp body closer to him. "You have always been a true warrior to us."

"No!" Christoff whispered as the ground disintegrated around his parents. "NO!" he screamed, lunging forward with his hand reaching for them as they disappeared into the open crevice. "NO! Please, Goddess, no!" he cried again, sobbing as he stared down into the deep abyss.

Rolling onto his back, he stared up at the mountain. He ignored the stinging embers of hot ash as they burned through his clothing. He no longer felt the pain from the rain of rocks and hot ash that continued to fall around him. He didn't even feel the burning of smoke from the numerous fires. Staring up at the mountain, he knew that he had to calm it. He also believed that he was the only one who could.

Pushing up off the ground, he called to his dragon and his symbiot. Shifting, he knew that he could not fly to the top of the mountain and ask for it to accept his life in exchange for the people of the village. Instead, he drew in a deep breath and began to run. He ran through the falling ash. He ran through the rain of rocks. He jumped over the deep crevice that stretched the valley. The closer he got to the mountain, the quieter it became.

When he reached the base of it, he started to climb. He climbed higher and higher with a determination, a focus, which defied his disability and air of frailty. His claws became bloody from the numerous cuts, but Christoff ignored that as well. When his dragon could not climb, he shifted and continued in his two legged form. His symbiot helped him, becoming a rope when he needed it and healing the deeper cuts so he could continue. By the time he reached the top, the mountain had grown quiet once again.

Christoff stood on a large ledge, looking down at the destruction to the valley, village, and his home. A wave of deep sorrow coursed through him. Unable to contain his grief, he tilted his head back and roared. In the distance, the villagers who had fled turned to the sound. They all heard the terrible sorrow in the haunting cry and they saw the small, frail boy-dragon standing at the top of the mountain. For just a moment, a glow of gold surrounded him, transforming him into a mighty warrior before he turned and disappeared into the once again quiet mountain.

CHAPTER ONE

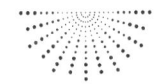

 resent Day:

Christoff sighed as he felt the rumble in the mountain. The activity inside it had been growing stronger each day for the past several months. He had traveled down through the numerous lava tunnels that had been created over the centuries to check on it. He knew each by heart since he had escaped to the top of the mountain when he was still just a boy.

His fingers dropped to his side and he gently stroked the golden symbiot pressed against his leg. It and his dragon had been his only companion all these long, lonely years. Several times he had tried to send his symbiot back to the hive where it had been created, but each time it refused to leave him, knowing that to do so would be certain death for him and his dragon.

"You should go," he murmured affectionately to his companion. "There is little time left for me and my dragon."

Images flashed through his mind of times when they climbed for hours to find a particularly good view of the valley far below. There were other times when his symbiot would sneak down to the valley and bring him and his dragon a special treat or new clothing that would cause some unsuspecting villager to wonder what had happened to it. An unfamiliar burning came to his eyes when he saw the vivid reminders of their days together.

"I want you...." Christoff shook his head and pushed past the symbiot to step closer to the mouth of his cave. He swallowed past the lump in his throat and glanced down at the golden creature given to him by the Goddess at his birth. "I want you to promise me you will go before the mountain wakes again. I fear I will not be able to calm it this time. I need to know that you are safe. Both my dragon and I need it, my friend."

Christoff turned when he heard a strange and unfamiliar sound carried upward by the wind. Tilting his head, he frowned and concentrated. It sounded like... younglings, very, very young younglings. His lips curved in a surprisingly amused smile when he caught what they were saying.

"I's tired," a young girl complained in a slightly grouchy tone. "I's not going to complain when mommy says it's nap-thirty no more."

"Me's neither," said the other one. "I's hope he's in a good mood."

Christoff knelt down and peered at the ledge as first one, then another small body came over the side. He watched in curiosity as one of the little girls rolled to her feet and put her tiny hands on her hips. He was able to catch a brief glimpse of a scowl on her face before she turned her back to him. It was obvious that she wasn't very happy.

"Who?" the girl demanded, looking at the other little girl as she climbed over and pulled a bag in front of her.

"The old dragon," the girl responded with an exasperated tone. "'Cause I might have to be like daddy and threatens to beat him up if he isn't."

Christoff bit back a chuckle and shook his head. Turning, he raised his eyebrow at his symbiot who was crouching beside him. It was in the shape of a large Werecat. It must have liked what it saw because its tail was flickering back and forth, as if in delight.

He turned his head back to stare down at the little girls. His fingers gripped the rock wall beside him when the mountain shook violently.

The little girl with the bag had risen just as the mountain began to shake. She took a step forward before falling backwards toward the edge. He knew immediately that she wouldn't be able to stop herself from falling over the side. Rising, he surged forward with a speed and agility born from centuries of climbing the steep cliffs of the mountain.

He reached up and over the one little girl to grab the other. His hand wrapped around the tiny wrist and he lifted her, careful not to harm her, into his arms. He started to reach for the other when their loud screams pierced the air. With a sigh of resignation, Christoff realized that not much had changed over the years.

Christoff tried to relax the stern expression on his face. He couldn't help but admit that he had been so fascinated by seeing the two unexpected figures and listening to what they were saying that he had forgotten the dangerous situation that they were in. He had been terrified when he saw the one young girl almost fall to her death. He stared down at the frightened, young face, trying to put his thoughts into words. He tilted his head and nodded when one of them spoke.

"You's the Old Dragon, aren't's you?" the first little girl that had climbed onto the ledge asked. "Wells? Aren't's you?"

"Yes, I guess I am," Christoff replied in a rusty voice. "Who are you and why are you on my mountain?"

"She's Amber and's I's Jade," the little girl in his arms said with a slightly superior tone. "We's gots more energys than the others, so's we's comes to finds you."

"Yeahs, we's needs your help," Amber responded.

"You should not be here," Christoff said, bending so he could set Jade down. "Where are your parents?"

"They is at homes," Jade said with a frown. "You's gots to goes helps our friends. They's hurt."

"Somes of thems are hurts," Amber corrected.

"How many?" Christoff asked in concern, motioning for his symbiot to shift and locate the other younglings.

Amber rolled her eyes at him and shook her head. "We's don't's knows 'cause we's don't's knows how to counts yet," she grumbled.

"There's Zohar and Bálint and Jabir and Alice and Roam and Spring and Phoenix and us," Jade said with a frown. "I's thinks that's alls of us."

"Go into the cave," Christoff ordered, walking toward the edge. "Go and don't come out. I will be back shortly with your friends."

He saw both girls nod their heads and turn to hurry toward his home. Fear swept through him with the knowledge that even there, they wouldn't be safe for long. The tremors were coming closer and closer together. He could only hope that the other younglings would be safe until he could reach them. After that, he didn't know what he would do.

Christoff focused on his symbiot. It had located several of the younglings and was moving down to several more. He carefully calcu- lated where he needed to step and grip to keep his balance. Within minutes, he had reached the section where a young girl with light blonde hair sat next to the still body of a young cub. Another young boy and a dark-haired girl sat protectively on either side of the other two.

Christoff had never seen a Sarafin cub in person before, but he had seen pictures of them. These younglings continued to surprise him, he thought as he jumped down onto the narrow ledge. His gaze swept over the unconscious cub. He quickly noted the boy's bloody paws and crooked tail.

"Can's you make the mountain quit shaking, please?" the little girl asked in a trembling voice. "It's scary."

Christoff watched as she continued to tenderly stroke the small furry head lying in her lap. He swallowed at the love and fear in the little girl's eyes. The only one that had ever looked at him that way had been his mother.

"He's hurt?" Christoff asked in a husky voice.

"Yes. He try to helps Jabir," she whispered. "I's thoughts Roams was goings to die. He's don't's knows it's yet, buts we's goings to always be's togethers. The goddess showed me we weres."

Christoff stared at the pair for a moment before he nodded. Glancing over his shoulder at the edge, he turned and walked over to the side. He knelt and looked down; three more younglings were on a ledge below him. His hands gripped the edge when the mountain trembled again, causing small rocks to rain down on the group below.

"Stay here," he ordered as he called to his symbiot.

They would need to hurry. He needed to get the younglings to safety. He could take them up to the top and have his symbiot transport them to the village. It would take precious time he wasn't sure that they had, though. Christoff focused on the huge golden eagle that his symbiot had shifted into as it appeared out of the clouds. With a silent command, it flew down and landed over the children. The symbiot protectively spread its wings to shelter them from the falling rocks.

Satisfied that the younglings were safe for the moment, he turned and swiftly climbed down to the lower ledge. He raised his eyebrow and smiled in amusement when the two young males growled at him when he stepped closer and knelt down next to the female. She looked so small and fragile that he hesitated for a moment before touching her.

His fingers brushed along the white strands as he gently stroked her pale cheek. "What happened?" he asked gruffly, turning his gaze back to the two boys.

"She saved me," one of the small boys replied in a voice trembling with fear and exhaustion. "It was too muches for her. She fell asleep and won't wakes up."

Christoff nodded before bending to carefully cradle the small figure in his arms. He paused, startled, when one of the boys stood up and pressed his small hand against his chest. His gaze locked with the boy's serious one. There was no doubt of the hint of warning in it.

"You's better not hurts her. I's Alice's protector," the youngling growled.

Christoff couldn't stop the smile. With a bow of his head, he rose to his feet. He wasn't sure where these younglings came from, but there was no doubt that they were very protective of each other.

"Rest easy, young warrior. I won't hurt your young charge," Christoff vowed in a tone that conveyed his determination to keep his word.

Making a decision that his cave was momentarily the safest place for them all, he knelt back down and nodded to the two boys. He needed to get them healed so that he could get them off the mountain. He wasn't absolutely sure how he would accomplish that, but he would find a way or die trying.

"Climb onto my back and hold on," he ordered before he shifted into his dragon form.

The two boys clung to his short wings as Christoff grabbed the uneven rock surface and began climbing, using just one arm, his back legs, and his tail to steady him. Once he was on the upper level, he ordered his symbiot to shift again, this time into a small transport. He laid the tiny girl in the seat while the two boys climbed off his back so they could sit next to her.

He didn't waste any time. Bending, he carefully picked up the Sarafin cub. His hand instinctively ran over the cub's head when it whimpered and turned to look up at him with frightened eyes. Swallowing, he smiled down at the cub in what he hoped was a reassuring manner as he carefully placed him in the transport as well. Turning, he helped the others in. It was all his symbiot could do to accommodate the small bodies.

"Take them to the cave," he ordered in a stern voice as he stepped back.

"What's about you?" one of the boys asked with a frown. "You's got to come too."

"My symbiot isn't as large as most warriors'," Christoff explained even as he started to turn away. "I will climb. It is not far. Go now."

CHAPTER TWO

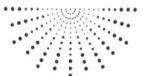

*C*hristoff realized as he climbed that no one was safe as long as they remained close to the mountain. He could not order his symbiot to take them to the village. They would need to be taken further away. He glanced down over his shoulder, gripping the rock face even as the mountain rumbled again. He wasn't sure if his symbiot could hold two more younglings, but it might not have a choice. There was no way he would let any of them be left behind.

It didn't take long for him to climb back up to the ledge leading to his cave. He quickly pulled himself up onto the flat shelf that protruded outward. Standing, he quickly strode into the dark interior that made up his home. He had ordered his symbiot to immediately begin healing the younglings as soon as they were safely inside. He wasn't sure if it would be able to, as it was smaller than most of the symbiots given to a warrior, but he knew that it would do its best.

Christoff jerked to a stop, staring in amazement at what should have been a dark, desolate area. He had never done much to the inside of the cave. It was where he slept, ate, and read. He had never found a need to decorate it. He lived on the top of a mountain with the beautiful view of the valley far below and the clouds above.

Now, he stood frozen in mid-stride, trying desperately to comprehend the transformation inside the dark walls of the cave. Slowly stepping forward, he gazed in wonder at the dozens of colorful lights that hung awkwardly along the jagged walls. Every corner of the cave was lit up by the brightly colored, battery-powered lights.

His gaze swept the room, pausing on the single table that he used for everything from carving to reading to eating. In the center of it was a small, pitiful-looking tree with round, colorful balls. It sat tilted at an odd angle and looked like it had seen better days.

Not unlike myself, Christoff couldn't help thinking abstractly.

He walked forward, his fingers sliding over one of the bright balls on the tree before touching a colorfully wrapped box. Beside it, on a chipped plate that his symbiot had brought back one day, sat a pile of sweets. He picked up the plate and sniffed it.

Almost immediately his mind flashed back to a memory of him standing in the kitchen with his mother. He had begged her to let him help, promising not to get in the way. He remembered her laughter as she carefully showed him how to stir the ingredients together. Afterward, they had sat out under the big tree with his father and ate the sweets with warm milk.

"What is this?" he asked, looking around the cave in confusion.

The first two little girls he had rescued grinned up at him. "We's brought you Christmas, so you's don't have to steals it," one of them informed him.

Christoff continued to stare around him, listening as the children explained what Christmas was when he told them he didn't know about it. The more they talked the more difficult it became for him to see and speak. They spoke of love and friendship. They spoke of accepting others that are different. His vision blurred when one of the little girls shifted. She was the most unusual, beautiful creature that he had ever seen with her long black feathers and too old eyes. Swallowing, he opened his mouth to speak when he heard a voice from outside the entrance to his cave, calling desperately for one of the younglings.

It was soon followed by others. He immediately realized that these were their parents. Not at home like the younglings thought, but searching frantically for their children.

Unsure of what to do, Christoff stepped into the shadows as several males and one female entered his home. He watched as they each bent to hug the younglings that fell into their open arms. With a painful twist, he realized that his time with these magical dragonlings was about to end. He turned to look at the female when she looked up at him as she lifted a small boy in her arms.

"Thank you," she whispered.

Christoff swallowed again and just nodded to her. He wasn't sure he could speak even if he wanted to. It was strange to see so many others of his kind after all these years. He moved uneasily when he saw all of the males turn to look at him. Bracing himself for their animosity, he was surprised when they looked at him with genuine... gratitude instead of hatred.

"We owe you more than we can ever repay," the Curizan male said, holding the fragile little girl with the almost white hair lovingly in his arms.

Christoff didn't know what to say at first. No one besides his own parents had ever thanked him before. Glancing at the colorful gifts and the tree, he awkwardly waved his hand at them.

"I... They have already repaid any debt," Christoff replied in a stiff voice. "They offered a gift no one else has ever given me."

One of the men he recognized as a member of the royal family bowed his head in respect before he looked at Christoff with concern. "The mountain is unstable," he said. "We need to evacuate."

Everything blurred as the mountain violently shook. Christoff's gaze caught the movement in the rock and he sprang forward, calling for his symbiot and dragon as a huge boulder started to shift under the massive tremor. He grunted as the boulder fell across his shoulders.

His legs trembled under the massive weight, but his gaze remained locked on the younglings and their parents.

He gritted his teeth, hearing the Curizan's words of encouragement as he helped him hold the boulder up long enough for the others to escape. Christoff was unable to respond, afraid to speak for fear of losing his focus.

We must hold the entrance open long enough for them to escape, he whispered to his dragon and symbiot. *We will not fail them. I will not let them die like I did father and mother.*

Christoff bowed his head, pushing upward far enough for the other men and the woman to escape with the younglings out onto the ledge. He groaned as the mountain shuddered, as if in protest that anyone would escape its anger. Christoff turned to order the Curizan to leave him. As he opened his mouth to speak, the boulder pressing down on them suddenly splintered, shattering into a million pieces and raining down on them like dust. The sudden release of the weight sent him to his knees as a wave of weakness and astonishment coursed through him at the power it would have taken to shatter a boulder that size.

"Let's go," the Curizan ordered in a harsh voice, pushing up off the ground.

Christoff rose shakily to his feet, bracing his hand along the rough wall of the cave. He shook his head in amazement. Turning to follow, he paused and glanced back into the area that had been his home for centuries. He didn't have much, but what he did have was precious to him: a few trinkets his symbiot had brought back from his childhood home, a locket that had belonged to his mother, and his father's carving knife. Those were the things that mattered the most to him.

His gaze froze on the two small presents the little girls had laid out on his table. Unable to leave the small items behind, he hurried back into the cave, snatching them off the table before reaching for the leather pouch he kept near the end of his bed.

He glanced around before turning back toward the entrance. A loud hiss escaped him when he felt his feet lift off the ground and his body flew through the air. His symbiot hit him around his midsection, driving him backwards and knocking the breath out of him. He landed on his long, narrow bed just as a large section of the ceiling collapsed where he had been standing.

Twisting on the bed, he barely heard the Curizan's shout of warning before the mountain shook with a tremendous force and an avalanche of rocks broke loose, sealing him in a tomb of darkness.

Several seconds passed before the air cleared enough for him to speak without choking on the dust. He pushed up on the bed. His dragon could see in very dim light, but not in pitch blackness.

"Give me light, my friend," Christoff whispered as a wave of resignation settled over him.

He felt his symbiot shake. He tried to give it comfort, but he knew he had very little left inside him to give to his dragon or symbiot. Christoff honestly didn't believe there was anything left that could heal his tired soul.

The faint glow from his symbiot was testament that it too realized that their time on this world was at an end. He rose from the bed and stepped around the crumbled remains of the ceiling of his home. Resting his hands against the rock covering the entrance, he whispered a soft farewell to the young dragonlings and their friends who had shown him compassion.

"It is better to have known such kindness before our death than to have never been touched by it at all, my friends," he whispered to his dragon and symbiot.

Pushing back, he straightened and turned. His symbiot was lying next to his bed, gazing at him with a look of sorrow and regret. He could feel the creature's feelings of guilt at not being big and strong enough to burst through the rocks and free them.

Christoff returned to his bed and his symbiot. He gently ran his fingers along its smooth head in comfort as he sent out a wave of warmth and affection to it. He would not let its final moments be filled with regret. Both he and his dragon understood and accepted that life was not always fair. It was what they made of it.

"Remember that, my golden friend," Christoff murmured as he continued to stroke the swirling gold body. "Mother and father accepted us and were proud of us. For centuries, we have done what we could to keep the mountain from erupting. It has grown as tired as us. The villagers have been evacuated. That is all that matters now. It is time for us to rest and hope that our worthiness as a guardian over the village will earn us a place as a warrior in the next life."

Christoff's head bowed as he whispered the last words. For centuries, he, his dragon, and his symbiot had fought to find ways to relieve the growing pressures inside the mountain. They had worked clearing old lava tubes and digging new tunnels to release the pressures building up. They had monitored the tremors and lava flows deep under the mountain. It had worked, but the pressure continued to build far deeper than any of them could go.

His gaze caught on the two brightly wrapped presents that were lying on the ground next to the bed. He had dropped them when his symbiot knocked him out of the way of the falling rocks. Reaching down, he picked them up, carefully balancing them in the palm of his hands before he set one down on his knees so he could open them.

He resisted the urge to rip the paper. Instead, he ran his finger down along the edge until it came free. He slowly folded the paper back to reveal the treasure hidden inside. The rumbling of the mountain and the increasing heat faded from his consciousness as the glitter of light from his symbiot caught on the delicately carved images of two dragons. He lifted one of them, noting that each dragon hung from its own chain. Holding them up, he realized that the two could connect together so that they looked like they were hugging each other.

Christoff glanced down, noticing a small piece of paper with beautiful, delicate flowing lettering on it. He picked it up, tilting it toward the dim light so he could read it. His hand began to tremble and the words blurred, but they would forever be etched into his soul.

As long as you hold your family and friends close to your heart, you will never be alone.

Lifting the necklaces, Christoff hooked each one around his neck. He picked up the empty box and set it on the table next to his bed. He gripped the edge when the mountain shook again, almost toppling the table. The air was beginning to thicken with an acidic smoke. He knew he was lucky if he had just a few more minutes.

"Please, Goddess, let me open this last gift. I have not asked for much in my life," Christoff whispered as he picked up the second box and again gently ran his finger along the paper so as not to tear it any more than necessary.

His eyes widened at the beautiful water-filled glass dome nestled inside the box. He lifted it up high enough to see the dragon and symbiot Werecat standing in front of a brightly colored tree. His gaze went to the pile of rubble. Under it lay the tree the two little girls had given him. Returning his attention to the dome, he tilted it and watched as white flakes floated down around the two figures. When he did it again, he saw a small lever on the bottom. He twisted the small piece of metal several times before releasing it. His home was suddenly filled with the delicate sounds of music. For a moment, he could imagine being back in his home in the valley as a boy, listening to his mother's sweet voice as she sang and his father played on his flute.

A sudden, overwhelming feeling of loneliness and depression swept over Christoff. Twisting the lever until it wouldn't turn any more, he held it up against his chest and lay back on the bed. Small tremors shook his body as grief and sorrow poured through him. For the first time in centuries, he cried for the loss of his parents. Not wanting to be alone, he patted the bed next to him. Warmth filled him as his symbiot jumped up beside him and laid down, resting its head against his flat stomach.

He reached down and caressed it. "Rest, my friend," he whispered, staring into the growing darkness as the light from his symbiot faded. "My dragon and I are tired, too. I think it is time to move on to the next world, what do you think?"

Another wave of warmth engulfed him as the light of his symbiot went out. He continued to stroke the small part of him that he had hoped would survive. No matter how much he tried to send it away, it would not leave him and his dragon. Christoff felt his dragon's grief, but also his acceptance that their time had come to an end.

"Rest well, my friends, for I have been the most fortunate of all to have you as my companions. No warrior could ask for better friends than you have been for the broken boy that I was or the man I grew to be. Sleep, it is time for us to rest," Christoff murmured before closing his eyes.

He could feel the mountain as it drew in a deep, calm breath before exhaling. He was surprised as he felt the pressure in the mountain exploding outward. He expected a flash of pain before death; instead, he was engulfed in a golden wave of warmth. A frown creased his brow before the tender touch of a hand brushed it away and he sank down into a silky abyss.

Aikaterina had remained behind after the dragonlings, Roam, and Alice's parents had rescued them. She had been curious when the old dragon had turned away from the entrance. She had planned to give his symbiot a touch of her blood to regain its strength so that it could help Christoff escape, but hesitated as a new thought came to her.

While her species normally tried not to interfere with the circle of life, she found it increasingly difficult to stay away from them. She had followed the dragonlings and their friends on their journey. They had each captured a special place inside her with their innocent love. It wasn't until she saw their gift of friendship and love that she knew she needed to help Christoff.

She had once again been torn when the entrance had caved in. It has been his symbiot's quiet plea for mercy for its friend and companion that had sealed her decision. The flashes of the old dragon's life had pierced her resolve. She remembered two other dragons, twin brothers who had felt the pull of the loneliness. It was in part her fault that they had never found their true mate. As her consciousness grew for this species, so did the understanding that she needed to help them if she could.

Floating down, she sat on the edge of the bed. Her gaze softened at Christoff's calm acceptance of his death. Lifting an invisible hand, she soothed it over his brow, knowing what she had to do.

"Not yet, my warrior," she softly whispered through his consciousness. "I hope you accept my Christmas gift to you."

CHAPTER THREE

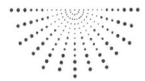

*E*dna Grey placed the box she had carried in from the shed down on the dining room table in the cabin that had once belonged to her friend, Abby Tanner. She had been shocked when the paperwork had arrived in the post from the attorney in Wyoming, giving her the cabin and surrounding land.

She knew deep down that she would always think of this as Abby's mountain. She had been friends with Abby's grandparents and had immediately been drawn to Abby when her mother had left her with them. Although she was in her mid-sixties, she knew she didn't feel or act it, a fact that drove her own daughter crazy at times.

Her hair was a beautiful white-gray with strands of silver through it. Shelly had grumbled that no woman in their sixties should have hair that thick and glossy. Edna couldn't help but smile as she remembered Shelly telling her about the problems Jack had after the last dinner they had attended with some of his friends. Supposedly, some of the men were asking Jack if Edna would be interested in going out with them. Edna had laughed when Shelly called to tell her about it. She seriously doubted that her son-in-law's lawyer friends would be interested in dating her.

Still, she couldn't help teasing her all too serious daughter. The memory of Shelly's reaction was priceless when she reminded her daughter that she was still alive and could appreciate masculine company just as much as Shelly did with Jack.

The "Eew, mom!" had quickly shut her daughter up. Of course, Jack's comment that if Shelly looked as good as her mom when she was her age had helped a little. Shelly had giggled and told him that he'd just have to wait to find out.

Edna chuckled when a curious nose pushed at her hand. Glancing down, she murmured to her Golden Retriever, Bo, to behave. Bo wagged his tail at her before sitting down to watch her.

"I think a little Christmas cheer will brighten the place up, what do you think?" Edna asked, pulling the small fiber optic Christmas tree out of the box to decorate the room until Jack and Shelly brought her a bigger one from town. "It's not as big as the one we normally put up, but it will do until Jack and Shelly get here. I wanted something to brighten the place up."

Bo barked and stood up, looking around for his green tennis ball. He scampered after it when it rolled across the hardwood floor. Edna laughed and decided that a Christmas tree needed Christmas music to go along with it. Walking over to where she had set up her old stereo system, she picked a classic from the pile of records and put it on.

She sang along with the songs as she worked to make the inside of the cabin look festive. She had decided to move into the cabin a few months ago when Jack, Shelly, and her granddaughter, Crystal, relocated from California to Shelby. As much as she loved her daughter, granddaughter, and son-in-law, she, Bo, and Gloria, her mule, were used to being on their own. Besides, the big house that she owned outside of town was nice, but it had become harder and harder to maintain by herself. She didn't entertain the way she used to, not like when Hanson had been alive.

Two hours later, Edna stood back and admired the colorful tree sitting on the table in the corner and festive garland decorated with red berries and poinsettias that hung over the mantle of the fireplace. Additional knickknacks added to the decor, giving it the final touch that it needed. A shiver ran through Edna when she glanced outside and saw that it was beginning to cloud up. The weather forecast predicted snow up here in the mountains. She would need to make sure that Gloria had fresh bedding for the night.

"Let me get the stew to simmering and we'll take Gloria for a walk up to the meadow for some exercise before it snows," Edna told Bo.

The Golden Retriever briefly looked up from the bone he was chewing on before returning his attention to it. The ever-present tennis ball lying by his left paw. Edna shook her head, thankful that Bo had outgrown his puppy stage early and at five years old, he was an absolute doll.

Twenty minutes later, Edna was bundled up for the cold. She had broken down and put on a pair of thermals under her faded jeans and added a sweater over the two shirts she was wearing. Sliding her feet into a pair of waterproof hiking boots, she grabbed her jacket, scarf, and wool cap off the peg by the door. Whistling for Bo, she braced herself for the frigid burst of air.

"Let's go, boy," she called, stepping back so Bo could go first. "I have to tell you, if you need to go out again tonight, you might just be going on your own."

Bo stopped at the bottom of the steps and dropped his ball so he could bark at her before picking it up again and racing toward the small stable and corral where Gloria now lived. Edna wasn't far behind him. She laughed and scolded Bo for getting under her feet when she tried to open the gate. Gloria, the old mule, lifted her head and watched for a moment before lowering her head back down to the ground again.

Edna walked over to the stable. She opened the sliding door and hooked it. She had debated whether she wanted to take Bo and Gloria for a walk first or prepare Gloria's stall. In the end, she decided she better place the fresh hay, water, and grain down first or she might not want to afterwards if it got too cold.

"Well, I have to say, it is certainly feeling like Christmas," Edna said to the mule and dog when they stuck their heads in the doorway and watched her. "I need to teach you two how to do this. I think you both are enjoying watching me work far too much."

Laughter filled the air when both animals backed out of the doorway and returned to the paddock. Shaking her head, Edna picked up the pitchfork and began spreading the straw. She sang as she worked.

Even after all these years, she still had her voice. She, Hanson, and Abby's grandparents had worked in the entertainment business for decades before retiring. Hanson had been in film while she had been in music. They had met at a premiere party for one of Hanson's movies and fallen in love at first sight. They had married six months after they met and had a wonderful forty years together before he passed away from a sudden heart attack five years ago.

Edna sighed as she finished spreading the straw. Replacing the pitchfork where it belonged, she picked up the two buckets she would need for the food and water. In a matter of minutes, Gloria's bed was ready for the night.

Edna grabbed the lead rope from the hook by the door and stepped out. She had already put Gloria's blanket on her earlier when the weather started to turn colder. Gloria trotted over to her when she saw the rope, knowing that meant they were going for a walk. Edna laughed again when Gloria nudged her gently with her head. She had nursed Gloria when she was barely a few hours old after her mother rejected her. Now, Gloria acted more like Bo than she did a mule.

"Well, at least you behave yourself with me," Edna said out loud. "Let's go up to the meadow and wish Abby a Happy Holiday. I'm sure she is sharing the holiday wherever she is. She always did love it. Who knows, maybe she'll send me one of her alien men as a present."

Gloria nibbled on the rope while Bo barked excitedly before picking up his tennis ball and racing for the path leading up to the high meadow. Edna couldn't believe it had been almost three years since Abby left

Earth to go to another world – an alien world filled with amazing and frightening things.

She had known deep in her heart that Abby hadn't died at the hands of the deranged Sheriff who turned out to be a serial killer. If she had any doubts, they dissolved when she received the letter from Paul Grove's friend and attorney, Chad Morrison. Chad had explained that Abby had sent back papers giving Edna the property she owned on the mountain.

Edna sighed as she walked along the path. She gazed around her at the forest. Some of the trees had lost all their leaves while others would remain green. Jack, Shelly, and Crystal had come up the week before with more boxes and stayed the weekend to help her clear the path and do some minor repairs on the barn and outside workshop.

Edna paused when she heard Bo's frantic barking coming from up ahead. For a moment she felt a sense of déjà vu sweep over her. Shaking her head at the crazy thought, she pulled on Gloria's lead rope.

"Come on, girl. Let's go see what Bo has discovered this time. I hope it isn't a bear that has decided to stay up for Santa," Edna chuckled. "I can just see it now. He'll probably be wearing one of those silly Santa hats, hoping for a pot of hon…ey. Oh, my!"

Edna's voice died as she jerked to a stop at the entrance to the meadow. Her eyes were glued to where Bo was barking and sniffing. Instead of a Santa cap-wearing bear, there was a golden capsule and if she had to make a guess, she bet there was an alien inside.

"Oh, boy!" Edna whispered, dropping Gloria's lead rope. "I guess I should be careful what I ask for."

CHAPTER FOUR

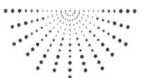

*E*dna drew in a deep breath as she approached the golden ship. She had seen one similar to it only once before, when Zoran, Abby's mate, had brought her up to the meadow to assure her that he would never harm her young friend. This one might be smaller, but it was made of the same material.

"Bo, come here, boy," Edna called out in a soft voice as she walked closer to the gold creature. "You're scaring it."

Bo released a whine and laid down next to the shimmering ship. Edna wasn't sure if it really qualified to be called a space ship. It looked barely large enough to hold one of the warriors, much less transport him anywhere. In fact, the closer she got to it, the more it looked like a type of coffin or one of those escape capsules from an alien movie set.

"It's okay, darling," Edna murmured in a soothing tone. "Bo didn't mean to upset you. You just startled him, that's all. I've seen one of you before. Zoran Reykill has a ship just like you. Do you know him?"

A smile curved Edna's lips when the creature shimmered and swirled, as if excited to hear Zoran's name. Pulling off her gloves, she tucked them in the pocket of her jacket before she reached out to touch the glowing surface. She hesitated just inches from it as a sudden wave of uncertainty swept through her. What if it wasn't friendly? What if she was misunderstanding the swirls as excitement, when in reality it was trying to warn her to stay away from it?

The decision whether or not to touch the creature was taken out of her hands when Gloria came up behind her and nudged her in the back, knocking her forward. Edna gasped as her hands splayed across the smooth surface. It took a moment for her to realize that she could see through the top. Her gaze remained frozen on the breathtaking man lying peacefully inside.

"Is he… alive?" Edna asked in a barely audible voice.

At first, she had been afraid to ask her question out loud for fear of discovering that the man was dead. Warmth filled her and an image of the man sleeping washed through her. Her hands curled against the silky smooth surface as she resisted the urge to touch him.

She started when she felt her hands sink into the surface of the ship. Frightened, she pulled them out and stepped back several steps. Raising a trembling hand to her face, she stopped when she saw the dancing threads of gold moving up her arms.

Edna giggled when the head of a tiny dragon appeared at the end of one of the threads and the long length shifted into a dragon's body and tail. It rubbed its head against her arm before winding around her wrists to form a bracelet. Shaking her head, she knew right then that it would never hurt her.

Stepping forward again, she stared down at the relaxed face of the man. He wasn't young like Zoran, but he was still breathtakingly handsome with silver strands running through his black hair. Her eyes widened when several flakes of white landed on the clear surface. It was only then that she realized it had begun to snow.

Glancing over at Gloria, she wondered what she should do. The golden creature was resting on the ground. If she could get it to move, she could take it back down to the cabin. There was no way she could leave it or the man out in the freezing cold. Turning back to the ship, she touched it.

"Can you understand me?" she asked in a soft voice.

Warmth filled her and she could see in her mind that it did. Breathing out a relieved sigh, she focused on trying to picture the cabin. She felt the ship shudder.

"It will be alright," Edna reassured it. "I just need to get you and your friend down to the cabin. There is a storm coming tonight and it's supposed to dump several feet of snow. You'll both freeze to death if you stay out here."

The creature shimmered and swirled again. Edna rested her hand on it and tried to think of the best way to get the capsule down the path to the cabin. Her first thought was the skid, but she'd never be able to lift the man onto it. What she really needed was a type of wagon.

Edna jerked back again when the creature shivered, then began to shift. A soft, amused laugh escaped her when four small wheels suddenly appeared just as Edna envisioned the type of wagon she would need. Shaking her head, she stepped behind the capsule and pushed on it. She was amazed at how easy it rolled. Calling for Gloria and Bo, Edna turned the golden wagon toward the path and began the slow journey back to the cabin.

"I really hope I know what the hell I'm doing because I'll be damned if he hasn't kicked my libido back into bloody drive by just lying there!" she whispered in exasperation as she glanced down at the male's face again.

It took a while, but Edna was able to get all five of them back to the cabin. She breathed a sigh of thanks that she had told Jack to hold off on removing the ramp Abby's grandfather had installed for her grandmother. It had come in handy during the move and she hadn't wanted to remove it until she felt confident she was through.

She had quickly tucked Gloria in for the night before closing the door to the stable and turning out all but one small heat lamp inside. Next, she opened the door to the cabin, sending another thank you to her old friend for enlarging the front door as well. Once inside, she shut the door and made sure that the pellet stove was on before she started a fire in the fireplace.

Removing her coat and hat, she blew on her numb fingers to warm them as she walked around the capsule now sitting on the rug in the living room. Stopping on the side, she gazed down at it with a frown. She reached out and touched the edge of the top, wondering how on earth she was going to open the damn thing.

"I could use a little help here," she murmured to the golden creature. "I'm not sure how I'm supposed to open it."

As if by magic, the top melted downward. Edna was caught off guard and started to fall forward. A loud gasp escaped her when a pair of arms suddenly wrapped around her and pulled her down onto the man's massive chest. Jerking her head up, she stared in fascination at the glittering gold eyes that were now wide awake.

CHAPTER FIVE

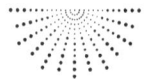

A strange feeling washed through Christoff as he slowly woke. He instinctively knew that he should be dead. He remembered the pressure of the mountain expanding outward right before he lost consciousness. There had been something else, almost like a hand against his brow, but he decided he must have been dreaming. One thing he did know, he should be dead.

Instead, he was encased in his symbiot. The familiar feel of his friend and companion sent a wave of comfort through him and his dragon. He was about to thank it for somehow, miraculously saving them when he felt a different type of warmth touch him. It felt as if someone had slid their hand over his body. Whoever, or whatever was touching him had definitely woken up his dragon. He had never felt his other half wake so fast or be so – focused – as it was now. Another slight caress washed across his body pulling a soft moan from him.

For a moment, Christoff kept his eyes closed, not wanting to lose the intense feeling of pleasure that was washing through his body. He knew the caress wasn't actually touching him; it didn't have to. As long as it was touching his symbiot, it was as if it was caressing his skin as well.

Curling his fingers, he focused on the movement of the creature as it walked around his symbiot. His body tensed as he waited for just the right moment to strike. He could see it was a female through the images his symbiot was sending to him. She looked similar to the one that came with the Dragon Lords back in the cave, only older... and definitely more beautiful to him. His opportunity came when the female stopped to stare down at him once more. He heard her murmur at the same time as he focused on his symbiot to release him.

The woman's soft, warm body fell into his arms as he reached for her. He drew her down until she was lying on top of him. His eyes swept over her face, noting the beauty of her silver hair and the startled look in her light green eyes.

"Uh, hello," she whispered, staring down at him. "I... Can you understand me?"

Christoff frowned. Yes, he could understand her. What he could not understand was his body's reaction to her. He felt...

Mine! his dragon roared in delight. *I bite. Yes, yes. I bite now.*

What? Bite? Why? Christoff asked in confusion as he continued to stare up at the woman.

She our mate! his dragon responded with a loud sigh.

"Mate!" Christoff exclaimed in shock, not realizing that he had spoken aloud until the woman's eyes widened in surprise and shock before a delicate blush rose up her cheeks.

"I... No, my name is Edna," the woman finally said with an amused smile.

"And my mate," Christoff replied with a confused frown.

Edna gently pushed against his chest, trying to pull free. He reluctantly released her, even as his dragon groaned and growled at him. He rose to a sitting position when she stepped back and slowly looked around. Everything was... different, alien.

"Where am I?" Christoff demanded in a husky voice, turning back to stare at the woman standing in front of him.

"You and your… ship are in my living room," Edna replied with a smile. "You are safe."

"Symbiot," Christoff automatically corrected as he pushed off the makeshift bed.

"What?" Edna asked in confusion this time.

Christoff touched his symbiot as it shifted into a large, strange creature. He started when he heard a noise and turned. Another beast, slightly smaller than his symbiot was lying on the floor, wagging its long, furry tail. His symbiot trotted over to it and pressed its nose forward.

"What is that?" Christoff asked, turning back to Edna.

She chuckled when the two golden beasts started to play. They were chasing a round, green ball across the floor. He could see them in his peripheral vision, but his main focus remained on the woman in front of him. The strange warmth invaded his body again, making him feel like a clumsy boy.

"Are you hungry?" she asked instead.

Christoff thought about it for a moment. His stomach rumbled. He couldn't remember the last time he ate.

"I… Yes," he finally said, suddenly feeling lost. "I do not understand what happened."

Edna's expression softened and she reached out to touch his hand. His eyes widened at the spark he felt when she touched him. It was strange and exciting and confusing all at the same time. Afraid she would disappear, he wrapped his fingers around her hand when she started to turn away.

"I put some stew on earlier. It should be done," she said in a comforting tone. "We can talk while we eat dinner. Does your – symbiot, I believe you called it – need anything to eat?"

Christoff shook his head as he glanced over to where his symbiot was lying. The green ball was between its front paws. The other beast was lying directly in front of it, softly whining. The furry creature's eyes were glued to the round toy. His symbiot leaned down and used its nose to push the ball toward it. He smiled when it turned to look at him and wagged its tail. A sense of happiness radiated from his symbiot.

He turned back around when Edna pulled her hand away while he was distracted. He stared in disbelief at her wrist when she reached up to push a strand of hair back from her face. His hand lifted and he gently touched the gold wrapped around it.

"My symbiot... does not need food like my dragon and I," Christoff murmured in a rusty, hesitant voice.

"Dragon...," Edna repeated, releasing a loud breath on the word. "I definitely think we have a few things to discuss."

Christoff nodded and followed her when she turned away. A crooked grin curved his lips as his gaze ran down over Edna, settling on her butt. The grin faded when she glanced over her shoulder at him. The raised eyebrow and flush to her cheeks told him the she was very much aware of where his eyes had been. He gave her a bashful grin when she shook her head and continued around the sitting area.

They entered the room behind it. He could tell it was the kitchen. His gaze shifted to a large pot on the stove and he drew in a deep, appreciative breath. He sure hoped she had a lot of whatever it was when his stomach and his dragon both growled in approval.

"You can sit down," Edna said, glancing at him. "I've told you my name, but you never told me yours."

"Christoff," he replied, standing to the side so he could watch her instead of sitting down like she suggested. "That smells good."

"Somebody is hungry," she responded with another soft laugh that echoed throughout the room when she heard his stomach emit a loud growl.

Christoff decided he liked the sound. He watched as she stirred the contents of the pot before ladling it into two bowls, one larger than the other. He reached around her and picked up the two, steaming bowls before she could.

"I'll get some crackers to go with it," Edna replied, shaking her head.

A few minutes later, the table was set and they were seated in front of the window where they could see the snow falling. Christoff studied Edna as she picked up several crackers and placed them on the small plate next to her. He hesitantly reached for several, giving her an uncertain smile when she looked at him.

A part of him wanted to grab the spoon and start shoveling the thick stew into his mouth. He couldn't remember the last time he'd smelled something so good. Instead, he waited for her to take the first bite. His father had always waited for his mother to begin eating before he started. He remembered asking his father why one evening.

"A warrior always cares for his mate before he cares for himself," his father had responded. "It is a small thing, but it shows my respect for your mother."

After that night, Christoff had waited as well. Lemar had made fun of him, but he hadn't cared. He wanted to show his mother that he respected her as well. He released a thankful sigh when Edna picked up her spoon and began to eat. Picking up his spoon, he filled it with the savory blend and lifted it to his mouth. He couldn't stop his eyes from closing as the delicious flavor washed over his senses.

Perhaps we did die in the explosion, he whispered to his dragon as it rolled over in ecstasy.

"I take it you like the stew?" Edna laughed.

Christoff's eyes popped open and he slowly pulled the spoon out of his mouth. A rueful smile curved his lips and he nodded. He waited for Edna to take another bite before he spooned a second serving into his mouth. This time, he kept his eyes focused on her.

"So, Christoff, tell me how you ended up on my mountain," Edna said after they had eaten most of the meal.

Christoff frowned and shook his head. "I don't know," he admitted. "I was trapped in the cave. The mountain was about to erupt. I felt it draw in its last breath before it did, then…."

Edna leaned forward and rested her elbows on the table, staring at him. He could see the worry and confusion in her eyes. He tried to remember the last few seconds in the cave, but all he remembered were the presents the younglings had left him. His eyes swept up in panic and he started to rise from his chair. He sank back down when his symbiot, sensing his distress and the reason for it, came into the small dining area with his leather satchel in its mouth.

Christoff reached for it, affectionately running his hand over the symbiot's head in appreciation. Placing the bag in his lap, he carefully opened the top. Inside, he could see his father's old shirt that he used to protect his precious memories of them. He knew that the carving knife and his mother's locket were inside it. On top, though, was the glass dome the two little girls had given him. He carefully pulled it out.

"The younglings," he started to say before his throat closed at the memory of their tender words. Drawing in a deep breath, he held the glass dome out to her. "They came to the mountain to find me."

Edna reached over and took the dome. He saw her eyes widen before she looked back at him. Her lips parted and tears filled her eyes as she gazed back and forth between it and him.

"This is Abby's work. I would know it anywhere," she whispered as a tear slid silently down her cheek. "Why did they come to find you?"

"They told me they wanted to be my friend so that I would not steal their Christmas," Christoff replied quietly, staring at the dome. "It has snow and on the bottom if you turn the small knob it will play music."

Edna smiled and nodded. He watched anxiously as she turned it over and twisted the small knob. The air was immediately filled with the song that Edna knew. His gaze jerked up when she began singing along with the melody. It was the most beautiful sound he had ever heard next to his mother's voice.

Edna gave a self-conscious laugh and brushed her hand across her damp cheek. Christoff rose out of his chair and walked around the table. He knelt by her chair and touched her cheek. His fingers spread across her soft skin, marveling at it.

"Who are you?" he asked with a confused frown. "My dragon says you are my mate. My symbiot has claimed you as well. And I…," he looked up into her beautiful eyes with a look of uncertainty.

"And you…?" Edna asked in a slightly breathless voice.

Christoff's eyes darkened to a deep gold as he leaned forward. "I find I can't keep my hands off you," he murmured, leaning forward to press his lips against her parted ones.

He marveled at the feel of her. This was the first time he had ever kissed a woman in all his long centuries of life. Oh, he had kissed his mother on her cheek, but he had never had an opportunity to kiss a female before, not like this. A burning ignited deep inside him. His body throbbed, making him ache with an awareness that he had been alone for far too long.

A silent curse escaped him when he felt his dragon pushing at him. Pulling back, he balanced himself for a moment on his heels before standing and stepping back. He needed to get control of himself. This was crazy! How he could even think that a woman such as Edna would be attracted to an old dragon like himself, one far past his prime, made him grimace.

"I…," he started to say.

Edna rose out of her seat and stepped toward him with a raised eyebrow. He clamped his lips together in a tight line when he saw the look of warning in her green eyes. Some instinct told him he had better not finish his sentence.

"So help me, if you say you regret kissing me, I'll pop you on the head with this globe," she hissed in warning.

Christoff's eyes widened in surprise before a delighted grin curved his lips. He shook his head. Reaching out, he took the globe from her hand before raising her fingers to his lips. Pressing a kiss to them, he stared into her eyes.

"I have no regret kissing you, Edna. In fact, I claim you as my true mate," he stated with a feeling of satisfaction. "You are now mine."

CHAPTER SIX

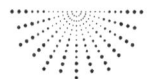

*L*ater that evening, Christoff knelt by the fireplace. He carefully arranged a few more pieces of wood on the fire. After dinner, he had helped Edna clean up the kitchen. His gaze flickered to the bedroom on the right before moving to the one on the left.

You let me bite, we no sleep in small bedroom no more, his dragon growled, pacing back and forth inside him.

What if I don't know what to do? What if we frighten her? What if..., Christoff grimaced when his dragon fell backwards, laughing.

I know what to do, his dragon assured him. *You let me bite, you will know too.*

She was very firm when she said that was our room, Christoff retorted.

We be even firmer, his dragon snorted. *I horny.*

You think I'm not? Christoff growled back.

"Are you alright?" Edna asked.

Christoff muttered a silent curse at his dragon when his dragon growled that *"No, they were not alright! They were extremely horny."*

Rising to his feet, a dark scowl crossed his face when he realized that if he turned around, Edna would be able to see the answer for herself. With a sigh of resignation, he turned to where she was standing in the hallway leading to the bathroom.

"I wish to share your bed tonight," Christoff said, wincing. "That was not what I meant to say."

Edna's eyes widened, her lips parted, and a rosy blush swept through her cheeks before she burst out laughing. Walking forward, she laid the towels in her arms down on the end table and stepped up to Christoff. Sliding her hands up his chest, she rested them on his shoulders to steady herself so that she could press a brief, hot kiss to his lips.

"I think that is the sweetest thing I have ever heard, but the answer is still no," she said with a shake of her head. "I've known you for approximately four hours. I think we need a few more before we decide if we should share a bed."

A flash of pain swept across Christoff's face before it cleared and a grin replaced it. She hadn't said "no", just that they needed a few more hours. By his calculations, that meant until it was bedtime. He could wait a few more hours.

You can, I can't, his dragon groaned. *I wants her now!*

Remember how father used to tease mother? Christoff replied as a plan of action formed in his mind. *He would brush his hands along her and give her kisses. By night, we could hear them. Mother could not resist father.*

You better be right, his dragon complained. *If not, I no kiss. I bite!*

If this does not work, you can bite, Christoff finally agreed.

"Christoff?" Edna called out, drawing him back to the present.

Christoff blinked and frowned when he saw that Edna was now by the front door to the cabin. His fists clenched when he saw she was reaching for her coat. His gaze flickered to the window. The snow was falling heavily now and there were already several inches of it on the window sill.

"Where are you going?" he demanded, taking a step forward. "The snow is falling and it is cold outside."

Edna chuckled and fastened her coat. "I know it's snowing, and yes, that means it is cold outside. I just want to check on Gloria before bedtime and Bo needs to go out once more before it gets too dark."

"I will go with you," Christoff informed her with a frown. "Who is Gloria?"

Edna paused and looked at him. He could see a flash of indecision in her eyes. He wondered if she was having second thoughts for a moment before he pushed it away. She had kissed him this time. He could still feel her warmth against his lips.

"You'll need a jacket. I think Jack left his here the last time he was up. I think it might fit you," she said.

"Who is Jack?" Christoff asked with a scowl. "I will fight him for you."

Edna paused by the door to a small closet off to the side and looked at him in amusement. Shaking her head, she opened the door and reached inside, pulling out a long, black coat. Shutting the door, she walked over to him and held it out.

"Jack is my son-in-law," Edna explained with a twinkle in her eye. "He would probably faint if you told him that you were going to fight him. Jack is good in a courtroom, but he is definitely more of a lover than a fighter. Hanson and I had one daughter, Shelly. I couldn't have any more after her. I started hemorrhaging and had to have a hysterectomy. Shelly and Jack only have one daughter, as well. My granddaughter, Crystal, is thirteen now."

Christoff reached for the coat, sniffing it. The scent of the man clung to it, but there were also other scents, too. They were softer, more delicate. He tried the coat on, surprised that it fit. His hands slid into the pockets and he discovered a pair of gloves and a hat. The gloves were too small, but he could wear the hat.

"Your mate was this Hanson?" he asked in a gruff voice as a feeling of jealousy washed through him.

He glanced down at Edna when she stepped closer to him. A small, sad smile curved her lips. She touched his arm, waiting for him to look into her eyes.

"He was my first love, my friend, my companion for many wonderful years and I will never regret having him in my life. It took me a few years to accept that he was gone and never coming back. We both made a promise to each other that if one of us died, we would grab life by the balls and live it to the fullest. I forgot that for a little while in my grief, but not any longer," she explained.

Christoff reached up and ran his fingers along her cheek. A sudden devilish grin curved his lips as he slid his hand around to her nape. Bending his head, he paused for a brief second.

"I think living life to the fullest would include me sharing your bed tonight," he murmured before he captured her lips.

Edna melted in his arms as he drew her up against his body. He deepened the kiss, sweeping his tongue into her mouth with an instinct born of need. A soft moan escaped her and he reveled in triumph when her hands slid up to tangle in his hair.

Several minutes later, they were both breathless. The only thing stopping them from losing themselves in the heat of passion was Bo's persistent whining. Christoff glared down at the Golden Retriever and grimaced.

"You pick a fine time to insist on going out," he muttered to the impatient dog. "The snow and cold weather better not dampen her desire," he warned.

Edna's laughter filled the cabin as she pulled on her woolen cap, scarf, and gloves. She gave Bo an affectionate pat on the head and glanced mischievously over her shoulder. Her lips and cheeks both a beautiful shade of red.

"If I get cold, I think I know someone who wouldn't mind warming me up," she teased, opening the front door so both Bo and Christoff's symbiot could escape out into the freezing weather. "Brrr! I think I'm definitely going to need some warming up tonight."

The grin on Christoff's face grew until a huge smile lit his face. Laughing, he stepped out and closed the door of the cabin. Grabbing Edna's hand, he closed his larger one around it.

"I can think of nothing better that I would like to do," he replied. "Now, tell me who this Gloria is."

CHAPTER SEVEN

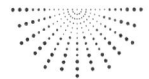

*E*dna couldn't remember the last time she had laughed so much. Her gaze followed Christoff as he played with Bo and his symbiot. She decided she needed to come up with a name for the creature. Another laugh escaped her when the symbiot turned to look at her as if knowing she was thinking about it and Bo tackled it, causing it to roll in the snow. Her eyes widened when it stood up and shook. Snow flew outward, coating Christoff and Bo. Tiny sparkles of ice crystals clung to its body.

"Spark," she murmured. "I'll call you Spark."

Warmth swept through her from the twin golden bracelets she wore, showing her that the symbiot was very pleased with its new name. Deciding that the three of them were having way too much fun, she bent to scoop up a handful of snow and formed a nice little snowball. Taking aim, she threw it, striking Christoff in the chest. A soft squeak escaped her when he turned in surprise.

"Oh, dear," Edna whispered, realizing that she might just have started something she wasn't sure how to finish if the heat in his eyes was anything to go by. "Christoff…," she started to say, backing up.

A soft gasp escaped her when her foot caught in the snow and she started to fall. She found herself wrapped in Christoff's arms before she could hit the ground. He rolled with her so that he was lying in the snow, not her.

"You must be careful," he whispered, gazing up at her.

"How did you move so fast?" she asked in wonder.

Christoff's expression grew serious. "I am not as fast as others of my kind," he admitted, turning his head to look at where his symbiot and Bo chased each other. "I am… smaller compared to other males of my species."

He turned back to look at Edna when she gently cupped his cheek. His breath caught in his throat when she bent her head to brush a tender kiss across his lips before raising her head to look at him again. There was a look of uncertainty in her gaze, but also something else, a tenderness that warmed his soul.

"I think you are perfect the way you are," Edna whispered, gazing down at him with a serious expression. "I've never liked men who were really tall. It is hard when every time you want to talk to them you have to look up. It gives you a crick in the neck. It's also harder to kiss them."

Christoff's gaze moved to her lips. "Do you try to kiss many of them?" he murmured.

"Only one, and he's just right," Edna replied, bending her head again.

She sighed as they kissed. They had kissed more in the past few hours than she had in the past six years! She felt like a horny teenager instead of a mature mother and grandmother. A moan escaped followed by a startled squeak when a very, very cold nose touched her cheek. Raising her head, she turned to glare at Bo.

"I swear you have the worst timing, Bo," she muttered before she remembered where they were. A look of dismay crossed her face as she realized that Christoff's backside was probably a Popsicle by now. "Oh, Christoff, you must be frozen."

He chuckled and slid his hand down to her hips, pressing up with his so she could feel him. Her lips parted in an 'O'. Well, at least that part of him wasn't cold.

"I think Bo is ready to go back inside," he said in a husky voice, grimacing when Bo tried to lick him. "The snow is falling harder and my dragon can sense a storm coming."

She didn't question how his dragon could sense the upcoming storm, she just trusted that it could. Scooting down him, she blushed when her hand dipped below his waist and she could feel the evidence of his desire still pressing against his pants. Rising, she held her hand out to him.

He rolled to his feet, grasping her outstretched hand once he was standing. Pulling her closer, he bent and swept her up into his arms. He ignored her protests as he stepped through the thickening layer of snow.

"I can walk," she protested. "I've lived in this area for years and can walk through a bit of snow."

He shrugged. "I want to carry you," he said. "I like you in my arms."

Edna bit back the desire to release a childish sigh of exasperation and roll her eyes at him. Instead, she relaxed back against his warmth. A sudden thought caused her to frown.

"You feel so warm," she said as he stepped up onto the porch.

Christoff bent his knees so he could open the door. He paused long enough to let his symbiot and Bo enter before he stepped in and closed it behind him. Only when they were standing in the warmth of the cabin did he set her back onto her feet.

"My dragon keeps me warm," he admitted. "I am also used to living high in the mountains."

Edna pulled her cap and gloves off, then unbuttoned her coat. She smiled her thanks when Christoff stepped around her to help her take it off. He hung it on the peg by the door before removing his coat.

"I tell you what," she said, walking across the living room. "You put more pellets in the stove and another log on the fire and I'll make us some hot chocolate and warm up some pie. Then, you can tell me about your mountain and I'll tell you about mine."

Christoff's expression clouded and a small pout pulled at his bottom lip, making him appear younger than his years. The twinkle in his eyes didn't hurt that image either, Edna thought as she turned away. If she wasn't careful, she would end up back in his arms and something told her the next time that happened, it wouldn't matter that they had only known each other for a few hours.

No, we'll be in the bedroom – together before the night is over if he keeps looking at me the way he is, she thought with amusement.

Walking into the kitchen, she pulled a small pot out and retrieved the milk. Within minutes, she was carrying a tray back into the living room with two steaming mugs of fresh hot chocolate and two pieces of apple pie with whipped cream, one slightly larger than the other, carefully balanced on the decorative platter. She bent and set the tray on the oval coffee table. Her eyes glittered with amusement when she saw Bo and Spark curled up on Bo's large doggy bed. Bo was passed out from all his playing and it looked like Spark wasn't far behind the Golden.

"Spark appears to have found a friend," Edna observed, handing Christoff a cup of hot chocolate and the plate with the pie.

"Spark?" Christoff frowned and looked over to where his symbiot lay contently next to Edna's furry creature.

She raised an eyebrow at Christoff. "I could hardly keep calling it your symbiot and I don't recall you calling it by a different name," she replied.

"I've never thought of naming it," he said, lifting the drink in his hands to his lips. His eyes widened in delight when the rich chocolate washed over his tongue. "This is very good. What is it?"

"Hot chocolate with whipped cream," she chuckled, watching as he licked the sweet, white cream off his upper lip. "Tell me about yourself, Christoff. Tell me where you come from," she asked in a husky voice.

"There is not much to tell," he replied.

Edna watched as Christoff's eyes dimmed. He took another sip of his chocolate, remaining silent. It was as if he was afraid to share his life. Deciding that maybe if she told him a little bit about her life that he might relax, she released a sigh and sat back on the couch. Taking another sip of her drink, she set it on the small side table before leaning forward to pick up her own plate as she tried to think of what to tell him.

"Mm, I've always had a soft spot for hot apple pie and whipped cream," she reflected. "Of course, anything goes well with whipped cream, if you ask me."

"Anything?" he asked, looking at the white, fluffy cream, then at her.

Edna waved her fork at him and laughed. "You have a very one track mind, my darling alien," she replied dryly before taking a bite of the pie.

"It's not that hard to have when I am near you," he muttered before bending his head to focus on his own dessert.

"You are amazingly good for my self-esteem," she replied. "Hanson was too in his own way. We met at a Hollywood party. Back then, it was all glitter, glitz, and an insane amount of money. The big studios held the world in the palms of their hands and musicals were still very popular. I had been hired as a singer in one of the new ones being produced with some of Hollywood's biggest names at the time. Abby's grandparents were working on the choreography and music while Hanson was one of the producers." She smiled as she remembered the days. "I don't miss it, but it was nice to have been a part of that era. He came to me and that was it. We spent the rest of the evening dancing and talking. We did that for almost forty years before he fell asleep one night and never woke up."

No longer hungry, she set the plate down on the small table next to her drink. She hated it when she got melancholic. Even though the memories were happy, they still hurt when she thought that Hanson was no longer there to share them with her. So many of her friends had either moved away, lost contact or passed away that she sometimes felt an overwhelming sense of loneliness inside her and she wondered what the future would hold for her. The one bright spot in her life was Shelly, Crystal, and Jack.

Christoff leaned forward and set his empty plate down on the table in front of him. Sitting back, he turned to look at her. She had that sad smile on her face again and her eyes glistened with unshed tears.

"You are lucky to have had someone," he murmured, reaching out to touch her hand. "I have spent centuries alone. Until today, I never really knew just how alone I was."

Edna looked at him in confusion. "Centuries? How is that possible?" she asked.

Christoff turned her hand over to stare down at her palm. He ran his thumb along the sensitive skin, noting how soft and delicate it looked against his own rough, scarred hand. He wondered how much to tell her, before deciding she deserved to know the truth about him before he claimed her.

No, after! his dragon roared, fighting inside him. *She not want me.*

She might… want us if she knows, Christoff replied in a hesitant whisper to his dragon.

She not, his dragon snarled with a shudder. *You see other girls in village. They make fun, laugh at us.*

She didn't laugh at me for being smaller than other males, he argued. *She said she liked my size.*

She not see little wings, his dragon mourned. *Her dragon no want me.*

"Christoff," Edna said in a gentle voice, touching his cheek. "What is it? I see… I see something running across your skin."

"My dragon, he is afraid," Christoff admitted in a soft voice. He released her hand and stood up to stand by the fireplace. He stared down at it for several long minutes before he turned to look at her again. "I was born premature. I should have died. I would have, if not for my mother and father's determination. Because of that, I was… different from the other younglings in the village. I was smaller, not as strong, and…."

He stopped and glanced at where Spark was on the bed next to Bo. His symbiot lifted its head and looked at him with sad eyes. He glanced at Edna before turning back to stare at the fire.

"And…," Edna asked, rising from the dark brown leather sofa.

Christoff swallowed and straightened his shoulders. He ignored the howl of his dragon as it circled inside him before lying down and burying its head in sorrow. Edna deserved the truth about him.

"My symbiot and dragon were smaller as well," he said, turning to gaze at her. "I was considered unfit to be a warrior, unworthy to be a true mate to a female. My dragon cannot fly. His wings never developed the way they should and cannot support our weight. I am… defective as a warrior."

Edna shook her head and reached up to touch his face. He turned his cheek into her palm and closed his eyes. It felt so good to be touched. He was terrified now that he had experienced what it was like to be with someone else, someone that made him feel whole, that it would be impossible for him to go back to the solitude that had filled his life before.

"I've already told you that I like you just the way you are," she said, gazing up at him. "Not too tall, not too short, just right, as Goldilocks would say. I've never seen a dragon, so I wouldn't know what to think in the first place."

"Would you… Would you like to see him? My dragon?" Christoff asked with an expression of uncertainty. "This way you will know what I am."

Edna blinked several times in surprise. He could see her hesitation and a mixture of fear and uncertainty. He braced himself for her answer even as his dragon roared at him in rage. He winced when he felt the sharp claws raking at his insides.

"Can you change… in here?" she asked, waving her hand at the living room. "I mean, aren't dragons supposed to be huge? Even small ones?"

Christoff frowned as he glanced around the living room. He would have to move the furniture, but his dragon would fit in the large, open room.

"I will move the furniture back, but I can fit," he assured her.

Edna released a soft breath and chuckled as she shook her head in disbelief. With a wave of her hand, she grinned up at him. He could see that she was scared, but she didn't say no.

No yet, his dragon growled in frustration. *She no want me. She no like me when she see me.*

We have to do this, Christoff ordered. *She deserves to have a choice.*

I no like you no more, his dragon snapped.

Christoff remained silent. He nodded to Edna and began moving the furniture while she picked up the dirty dishes and took them to the kitchen. He could hear the water running as she washed them. Glancing at his symbiot, he released a deep breath and called to his dragon. It took several tries before his dragon finally responded. His eyes closed as he felt the familiar change sweep over him.

He remained frozen, his eyes closed against the rejection he and his dragon were positive they would get. He would not blame Edna if she did. None of his own kind accepted him except his mother and father.

An image of the dragonlings flowed through his mind, as well as their parents. Surprise flooded him when he realized that they had accepted him. Another image, this time of the small black dragon with the beautiful feathers surfaced and the face of her father holding her. All of the other dragonlings and their two companions had also looked beneath her differences to the soul captured inside.

His eyes slowly opened and he stared at Edna. She stood gazing at him in awe. His eyes followed her trembling hand as she raised it to brush a strand of gray and silver hair back from her face. His dragon trembled as well when she took a step closer to him.

"Can I touch you?" she asked in a faint voice.

Christoff snorted and slowly nodded his head. He lowered it when she reached up to touch his snout. While he was smaller than the typical dragon, he was still taller than her. He started when his dragon blew a puff of warm air around her hand.

Edna's soft giggle pulled at him. He rubbed his nose affectionately against her palm before swiping it with his tongue. Another burst of laughter echoed in the room. That was something he was learning about Edna; she liked to laugh.

"You are so beautiful," she whispered, stroking his head and jaw.

His eyes drooped when she carefully traced several scales along his jaw. Releasing a playful sniff, a pleased moan escaped him when she ran her fingers along his left nostril and up his snout to his brow. The pleasure turned to an uncomfortable rumble of unease when she ran her hand down along his neck to his shoulder. She would see his deformed wings. Turning his head, he studied her expression as she looked at them.

A low growl of warning escaped him when she started to reach out to touch them. Her hand froze and she turned to look at him. Licking her lips, she drew in a deep breath and continued to reach out.

She going to touch them, his dragon groaned in despair. *She see them.*

Yes, Christoff whispered. *She sees them.*

Deep down, he braced himself for her rejection while another part of him rejoiced that she hadn't shunned him – yet. Excitement began to build when he felt her hands stroking his small wings. He tilted his head when she carefully lifted one.

"You are the most beautiful creature I have ever seen in my life," she whispered, shaking her head in astonishment. "Why you would be worried about whether I would accept you in this form is beyond me. You are incredible."

Christoff swung his tail around, wrapping it around Edna and twisting so that he could run his tongue up her cheek. Her choked laughter filled his soul with wonder as she wrapped her arms around his head and pressed a kiss between his eyes. Unable to stop, he shifted back into his two legged form, catching her when she swayed.

"You are definitely mine," he whispered in a dark, husky voice filled with emotion.

CHAPTER EIGHT

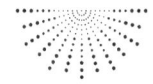

*L*ater that evening, Christoff stepped out of the shower in the guest bedroom. He stared moodily at the large bed. The large, empty bed, he thought with regret.

"I'm not happy about it either," he grumbled when his dragon snorted in disgust.

"Christoff, I thought you might like to wear... Oh, my," Edna whispered, standing in the doorway staring at Christoff's nearly naked body. A soft groan escaped her. "There ought to be a law against men your age looking this good."

Christoff turned when he heard Edna. A slow, sexy grin curled his lips. He raised an eyebrow and his fingers moved to the towel wrapped around his waist. He wasn't above playing dirty if it would keep him from having to spend one more day in his long life alone.

"Are those for me?" he asked innocently as he started to loosen the towel where it was tucked in against his flat stomach.

"Don't... Don't you dare!" Edna hissed in a slightly hoarse voice. "Christoff, you wouldn't... Oh, damn, you would!"

Christoff let the towel he was wearing fall to the floor. He was so turned on that the towel wouldn't have covered his desire anyway. Besides, Edna might as well know the effect she was having on him.

"It is warm in here," he replied, stepping closer to her. "The only thing that would keep me warmer was if I had you next to me."

He saw Edna swallow, her gaze glued to his arousal. A wicked grin curved his lips when he felt his cock react to her appraisal and jerk upward. The low hiss that escaped her showed that she wasn't immune to his body.

"You are very…," she started to say, forcing her eyes up his body until they collided with his dark gold ones. "You did that on purpose."

Christoff chuckled and stepped closer. "Yes, I have decided I've spent enough of my life alone. I do not wish to be alone ever again." His voice softened and he grew serious as he reached up to touch her cheek. "A true mate is a gift from the Goddess, Edna. A warrior knows when he has found his."

"How? How can you be sure?" she asked, staring up at him.

He ran his hand down her arm and lifted her wrist so she could see one of the gold bracelets wrapped around her wrists. He leaned down and pressed a kiss along the edge of it. His eyes darkened when he felt her pulse jump.

"All three parts of a Valdier warrior must accept a female for her to be his true mate. My symbiot has claimed you. It would not have given you these if it had not. My dragon claws at me to bite you. And, I… Since you fell into my arms early this morning, I have not been able to resist touching you. This is a gift, Edna, one that I will fight for."

Edna's eyes closed for a moment before she opened them. Pulling away, she turned and walked over to the dresser, setting the sweat pants that she had found down on the dresser. Turning back around, she stared at Christoff with a small smile.

"I'm not as slim and trim as I was in my youth. My breasts aren't perky, my stomach isn't flat, and my hips a bit wider than they used to be," she said with a self-conscious laugh. "I haven't been with a man in over five years, but if you don't care that I'm not as young as I used to be, I'd love to have you next to me tonight – and every night after."

Christoff released a deep sigh and nodded. He stepped forward and gripped the hand she held out to him. Together, they walked through the living room and back to her room. He forced down the wave of panic building inside him, wondering if he should tell her that he had never been with a female before.

NO! his dragon snapped. *You leave this to me. I know what to do.*

You haven't been with another dragon before, so how are you supposed to know? Christoff grumbled silently as Edna released his hand and pulled at the tie wrapped around her waist.

You be quiet! his dragon insisted. *I no want to scare her off.*

"Edna," Christoff whispered in a hoarse voice as she shrugged her robe off and tossed it onto a nearby chair.

She turned to look at him. He could see the uncertainty in her face and knew she was thinking he was having second thoughts. He could never let her think it was her.

"I understand if you've changed your mind," she said with a slightly embarrassed laugh.

"You said it had been five years since you had been with a man," Christoff started to say, cupping her cheek so that he could force her to look at him.

"Yes," she replied.

"I have never been with a female before," he admitted in a gruff voice. "Will you teach me?"

For a moment, Edna didn't think she had heard Christoff correctly. Tilting her head, she stared at him with a frown. Did he just say he had never been with a woman before? Surely, she must have heard him wrong.

"I beg your pardon? Did you just say you've never been with a woman before?" Edna asked in a slightly higher voice than she intended.

Even in the dim light cast by her bedside lamp, she could see his cheeks turn darker. She blinked several times, trying to understand what he'd really just said. She must have misunderstood him. There was no way he could be a – virgin, could he?

"Yes," he admitted with a wince. "My dragon said I should not have told you that."

A wild giggle escaped Edna and she had to cover her mouth to keep it in. She was a sixty-five year old woman standing in the middle of her bedroom talking to an alien male who was not only a virgin, but arguing with his dragon about whether or not he should have admitted it. To top it off, he wanted her to teach him how to make love. This was almost as bad as her honeymoon, only in reverse.

"I… I'm sorry," she whispered as another nervous giggle escaped her. "It's just… This is a first for me."

Christoff scowled and folded his arms across his chest. "It is for me as well, which is why I told you," he said, lifting his chin.

"Yes, of course," Edna muttered, fanning herself and wondering if she was about to start having hot flashes again. "I… need a moment."

She needed more than a moment, she needed a stiff drink. A virgin. Hell, the only virgin she had ever known was her! Well, and Shelly. She hadn't exactly handled that discussion very well either. Hanson had to come in and take over. If she remembered correctly, that discussion had involved a bottle of wine and a lot of embarrassed giggles.

"How long of a moment do you need?" Christoff asked curiously. "My dragon wants to know."

A slightly hysterical laugh escaped Edna. "Is he… Is he going to be with us the entire time?" she asked, trying to keep a straight face.

"Of course," Christoff replied. "He is a part of me and he will be part of our mating."

"Great, a ménage," she whispered. "The night is just full of firsts for all of us."

Christoff gazed down at her in confusion. "That is a good thing?" he asked, tilting his head when she laughed again. "It is something you will enjoy, yes?"

Edna blew out a loud breath and smiled. "As you so eloquently said this is a night for firsts. I'm sure we'll have a wonderful time together – all three of us. Spark isn't going to be joining us, is he?" she asked faintly, lifting one hand to her throat.

Christoff frowned. "I can ask, if you would like," he said.

"No! No, that is alright," Edna whispered, shaking her head. "I think the bed will be crowded enough as it is."

"So, what do we do first?" Christoff asked, dropping his arms to his side.

Edna's eyes jerked up to his face. A light laugh escaped her at the excitement on it. She suddenly felt young and wild and free. Reaching down, she grabbed the bottom of her nightgown. She was going to have to invest in something a little sexier than her flannel shorty. Pulling it over her head, she tossed it to the side before stepping up to run her hand up Christoff's broad chest.

"Now, we kiss," she murmured, pressing him back until he sat down on the edge of the bed. "And just take it one touch at a time."

CHAPTER NINE

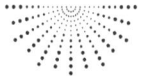

Christoff wound his arms around Edna, pulling her down on top of him as he lay back against the pillows. His mouth opened and he hungrily devoured her kisses like a dying man taking his last breath. He didn't know how he had come to be in this strange magical world. If he was dreaming, he hoped he never woke up. This was his next life. His body might not be whole and undamaged, but it didn't matter anymore. All that mattered was that he had finally been given a true mate, his partner in life, after so many centuries.

His hands moved down to her hips and a soft moan escaped him as he pressed himself upward. He could feel the waves of dragon fire building inside him, desperate to get out. Breaking their kiss, he ran his lips down along her jaw.

"Oh!" Edna whispered when he nipped her.

"I want to touch you," he murmured against her skin. "All of you."

Edna leaned back far enough to look down at him. A tender smile curved her lips. He looked like a little boy at Christmas who didn't know which present to open first.

"I think that is a wonderful idea," she said with a slightly unsteady smile. "I wouldn't mind exploring all of you, too."

Christoff rolled so that they were lying side by side. He gazed into her eyes, trying to note what brought her the most pleasure as he ran his hands over her. His fingers trailed over her hip and across her stomach. He paused when he encountered a small patch of soft curls. Curious, he gently pushed her over onto her back and sat up.

"You are soft," he observed, trailing his fingers through the fine hair. "I like that."

Edna gave a choked laugh and shook her head. "I'm glad. I've kept a bit of my figure with the help of yoga, but it's not what it was when I was younger," she retorted in a teasing tone. "Are you sure you've never done this before?" she added with a shudder when he ran his finger along her sensitive nub.

"You like this. I can see your face flush and your heart is racing," he replied with a grin.

"Let's see how you handle me exploring you, my curious alien," she retorted with a sly smile of her own, deciding she could do a little playing, too.

Christoff's eyes widened and he sucked in a deep breath when Edna suddenly sat up and wrapped her hand around his throbbing cock. The next moment, he was panting. She was running her hand up and down his cock, from the base of it to the head and back again in long, slow, agonizing strokes.

"Edna," he groaned.

"Lay down, Christoff," she whispered, turning as he did so. "I think this first time should be about you."

He shook his head. "It should be about us, Edna," he said hoarsely. "You are my true mate. You will always come first."

Edna chuckled. "Not this time, my alien virgin. This time, it is all about you," she teased, lowering her head to kiss him.

Christoff leaned upward into her. Her lips teased his skin just as her hand stroked his cock. He released her hips to grip the covers when she began moving down his body. A light sweat broke out on his brow and he stared up at the ceiling, wondering when she was going to stop and hoping that she never did.

"Edna!" he choked out when he felt her warm, moist mouth cover the end of his cock. "Great Goddess above!"

His gaze remained frozen at the sight of Edna's lips wrapped lovingly around his cock. He could feel the heat building inside him. His dragon was purring so loudly he was surprised that Edna couldn't hear him!

His hips began to instinctively rock to the same rhythm of her head. The feel of her long braid against his inner thigh was like someone stroking the fire until it ignited with such a force he was left gasping for air. His body stiffened and he swore the mountain was trembling again as he came.

It took several minutes for him to realize that he was still alive. Forcing his stiff fingers to release the covers, he reached with shaking hands to caress Edna's hair. A shudder ran through his length when she slid her lips from around his cock with a soft moan of pleasure.

She smiled up at him with her rosy lips. He leaned forward and wrapped his arms around her. Lying back, he raised his hand to cup her chin. He kept their eyes locked on each other as he leaned up to kiss her. He could taste his essence on her lips. The memory of what she had just done reignited the fire in his gut.

"Now, it is my turn," he growled, rolling over until she was trapped under him. "I will do the same to you."

"Christoff!" Edna gasped, stunned when he began moving down her body with an ease that belied his experience. "Are you sure you've never done this before?" she moaned, grasping his shoulders when he began sucking on her nipples. "Oh, yes! Oh, yes!"

Christoff decided right then and there he would always start by kissing her, one inch at a time. He turned his attention to her other nipple. It had grown hard and full as well. It made it easier for him to pinch them between his fingers.

He soon discovered that the more he played with them, the louder she cried out and wiggled. His cock was throbbing again and he wanted, needed to drive it into her. The thought shocked him.

Focusing on his first intention, he worked his way down over Edna's stomach to the soft curls between her legs. She immediately arched upward and parted her legs further for him. The sweet scent of her arousal made his mouth water. He wondered if she tasted as good as she smelled.

"Sweet orange spice," Edna cried out. "Oh, Christoff!"

Christoff had no idea what sweet orange spice was, but he did know that when he parted the soft skin protecting the nub he had found earlier that she definitely liked it. He parted the protective skin and ran his tongue over the nub, enjoying how it swelled at his touch.

Yes, you lick, I bite, we do good, his dragon crowed in delight. *My mate! I get my mate.*

Christoff tried to push his dragon back, but the damn thing was determined to have his way this time. He could feel the dragon fire building inside him until he thought he would explode as the pressure built to unbearable levels. Instinctively, he knew what it was and what he needed to do. He just wasn't sure what would happen once he did it.

I bite, now, I bite, his dragon growled.

Christoff felt the scales of his dragon rippling up his neck and over his shoulders. He fought for control, but his dragon wouldn't have any part of it. They were both too far gone in their need for their mate. He felt his teeth extending and knew that tonight, he would have his mate.

Or we die, his dragon moaned.

Die?! What do you mean we die? Christoff choked out even as he felt his head turn and he sank his teeth into Edna's thigh.

Her startled cry tore at him, even as he breathed the dragon fire into her bloodstream. He could feel it pumping into her. She started to fight against him before a loud moan escaped her and she began to writhe in his arms. Sliding his hands up under her thighs, he kept her open to him as he continued to breathe the fire of his dragon into her. Only when he felt the last of the fire pour into her did he run his tongue over the mark he had left. If the Goddess thought them worthy, a new dragon would be born tonight. One that would heal his fractured soul.

Christoff turned his tortured eyes to Edna. "You are mine, Edna. I claim you as my true mate. No others may have you. I will live to protect you. You are mine to love, to protect, forever," he murmured, knowing he would say the words to her over and over before the night turned to dawn.

Bending forward, he clamped down on the swollen nub and sucked hard, at the same time inserting two fingers up into her slick vaginal channel. He could feel her pulsing around him. Her need was growing as the heat of the dragon's fire swept through her.

He felt it when the first wave hit, sending a shattering orgasm through her that left her shaking and gasping for air. Rising up, he slid back up her body, touching and kissing each part as he went. His own body was hard and throbbing with need. Tonight, he would fill her with the essence of his dragon.

"I need you, Edna," he groaned, holding his body over her.

Edna's legs parted and she reached between them, guiding him into her. She stared up at him with wide, light green eyes filled with need. Her lips parted, but he could sense the next wave rising up. Bending, he captured her cry at the same time as he drove himself into her. The combination proved to be the catalyst needed to bring the wave to a crest and it burst around them, soaking them in a fire that would last the rest of the night.

Edna jerked awake, disoriented for a moment. Her body felt like it was on fire. This was nothing like the hot flashes she had gone through. They were a piece of cake. No, this was a full-fledged inferno.

Her body arched as another wave hit her. She could feel hot moisture pool between her legs. A soft moan escaped her and she rolled, coming up against a hot, solid body. Christoff! She didn't know what he had done to her, but she felt like she would die if he didn't take the edge off the heat. Sitting up, she slid her leg over him so she could straddle him. She lifted up, just high enough so that his hard cock could seat itself in her slick channel.

"Edna," Christoff whispered, coming awake immediately. "The fire..."

"It burns, Christoff," Edna moaned, bowing her head as she splayed her hands across his chest. "I need you to put it out."

Christoff gripped her hips to hold her steady as he pressed upward at the same time as he drew her down on top of him. She could feel every exquisite inch of him as he impaled her. Never in her life had she wanted, needed someone the way she needed him. There was nothing human in their mating. It was all primitive need as she began riding him with an energy she hadn't felt in years.

"Yes, my beautiful mate," Christoff whispered, staring up at her in wonder. "Come for me. Tonight a new dragon will be born."

Edna was vaguely aware of the pale green marks running up her arms. She thought they were a product of her imagination. After all, she didn't have scales. Christoff had scales – beautiful ruby and silver scales that danced over his skin when they made love.

Her body shook and her heart stuttered for a moment as the fire increased. She could sense Christoff pulling her closer, but everything was blurred. Her heart was pounding too fast, too hard. In the back of her mind, she was afraid she might be having a heart attack. She was having trouble catching her breath.

"Christoff?" Edna whimpered as he tilted her head to the side.

"Accept me, Edna," he whispered. "Accept our dragons."

"Yes," she moaned, crying out when he sank his teeth into her again, this time along her neck and started to breathe the flames to life again.

Fire seared her veins, and the transformation that had started hours ago burst outward, finishing the change to her blood, her organs, her very essence. Deep down, another spark suddenly burst into life. It flickered for a moment, almost going out, but the low, mournful cry of a male dragon pulled at it, fanning it until it flickered back to life.

My true mate, his dragon breathed, watching as his mate was born.

CHAPTER TEN

*E*dna glanced up from where she was preparing a late breakfast the next morning when she heard Bo bark in excitement. For a moment panic hit her. She had forgotten that Shelly, Jack, and Crystal were bringing her a Christmas tree today. Her eyes flew to the back bedroom where Christoff was still sleeping. She had gotten up to let Bo outside so he could take care of his morning business and to feed Gloria.

"Bo, hush," she ordered, biting her lip. "Behave. Spark, you too! Go to Christoff."

The symbiot had risen off of the rug in front of the fire and had shifted into a large beast that Edna swore was a cross between a lion and a sabretooth tiger. It was staring at the door, emitting a low growl. She could just imagine Jack and Shelly's faces if they came in and saw it.

Wiping her hands, she walked over to Spark and touched him. The symbiot immediately calmed under her hand. Warmth filled her as it responded to her gentle stroking.

"It's my family, Spark. I need you to go to Christoff, stay with him until I call you. I need to explain you and Christoff before they see you," she explained. "Please."

Spark snorted and shook his head before reluctantly turning toward the bedroom. Edna breathed a sigh of relief. Wiping her hands along her jeans, she listened to the sound of car doors shutting. She glanced back at the bedroom one last time before she opened the door.

"Hey, Mom," Shelly called out.

"Hi, Edna," Jack said as he began loosening the ropes holding the Christmas tree onto the roof of the SUV.

Edna's expression softened as she watched her thirteen year old grand-daughter struggle for a moment in the thick snow. She rubbed her hands together at the biting cold and watched as Bo raced over to see what Jack and Shelly were doing.

"Come on in, Crystal," Edna said with a smile. "Are you enjoying the snow?"

Crystal made a face as she walked by. Edna released a sigh. Crystal was going through a difficult time. The few times she had gone down to the house, Shelly had complained that Crystal's moodiness was getting unbearable.

"It's okay. It's kind of hard to walk in," Crystal mumbled as she walked past Edna.

Edna nodded and turned to follow Crystal into the house. Closing the door, she helped Crystal with her coat. Crystal bent awkwardly to remove her boot.

"You have a new prosthetic," Edna noted, seeing the space-age-looking lower limb on Crystal's left leg.

"Yeah, I got it last week. It's going to take some getting used to," Crystal replied with a shrug.

Edna nodded. Crystal had lost her left leg in a car accident that had killed her best friend and her friend's mother two years ago. Since then, she had transformed from a sweet, outgoing young girl into a solemn one. She seldom left the house anymore. Edna had been hesitant when Shelly mentioned that she would be homeschooling Crystal, afraid that it would encourage Crystal to withdraw even further into her shell. The only thing that seemed to help was her granddaughter's love of music.

Edna turned when the door opened and Shelly and Jack came in carrying the tree. A shiver escaped her as a gust of icy air swept in behind them. Bo followed, shaking snow off of his coat and sending icy droplets everywhere. She closed the door and hurried to the kitchen. Grabbing a dishtowel, she quickly mopped up the melting snow off the floor so it wouldn't be slippery.

Her gaze swept to the now closed door of the bedroom. She hoped that Christoff stayed in the room long enough for her to explain him to her family. Returning to the living room, she nervously smiled at her daughter as they straightened the tree.

"That is a beautiful tree. How was the drive up the mountain? It can be a bit harrowing sometimes," Edna commented, wiping up the water.

"It wasn't as bad as I thought it would be. It looks like one of the snow-plows had come up it earlier," Jack replied, bending to tighten the screws on the stand. "We made it to the Christmas tree store first thing. Crystal helped us pick it out."

"Hopefully, she'll help us decorate it, too," Shelly added, glancing at where Crystal was sitting on the couch playing on her cell phone.

"Yes, well, that would be wonderful. How long are you planning on staying?" Edna asked, glancing toward the bedroom again. Had she heard a noise? "I forgot to get the decorations out of the workshop."

"I'll go get them," Jack said.

"That would be wonderful," Edna said with a relieved smile.

"Come on, Bo. You can help me," Jack said as he adjusted his hat.

Edna watched as Jack disappeared back outside. Breathing a sigh of relief, she turned to look at the tree. Instead, her attention was caught by her daughter's stern expression.

"What's going on? I haven't seen you this frazzled since you and the red hat ladies got drunk at the Golf Resort last Christmas and had to call me to pick you up," Shelly said, folding her arms across her chest.

"Why would you think anything is going on?" Edna asked, lifting her hand to smooth her hair back from her face.

Shelly looked critically at her for several long seconds. Edna grimaced and looked away. She had forgotten what it felt like to be a teenager.

"You have your shirt on inside out," Crystal commented without looking up. "And you have a hickey on your neck."

"I have a...." Edna's eyes widened and she could feel her cheeks heating.

"A hickey! Where?" Shelly demanded, stepping closer to her mom.

Edna covered the mark on her neck and glared at Crystal who ignored her. She winced when Shelly reached up and pulled her hand away. Stepping back, she straightened her blouse, noting that Crystal was right, it was inside out.

"I... There's something I need to tell you," Edna began.

Things would have gone much better if both the front door and the bedroom door hadn't opened at the same time. Edna didn't know which way to look first. She heard the box Jack was carrying hit the floor at the same time as Bo barked, Shelly gasped, Crystal released an exclamation that sounded suspiciously like "Whoa, hunk alert!", and Christoff emerged from the bedroom.

"Mom?" Shelly squeaked, stepping backwards and running into Jack.

"What the hell?" Jack muttered, staring in disbelief.

"Whoa, grandma! Nice boyfriend material," Crystal breathed, looking at Christoff in awe.

Edna glanced back and forth between everyone before finally throwing her hands up in the air. She glared at Christoff. He just grinned at her with that damn smile that melted her heart.

"I need some coffee – with a shot of whiskey in it," she growled, turning on her heel and heading for the kitchen.

"Mom?" Shelly yelped.

Edna turned and looked at her daughter with an exasperated sigh. "This is Christoff. He's… staying with me," she stated before walking into the kitchen.

Edna could hear Jack clearing his throat. The prosecutor was coming out, she thought in resignation. Christoff was about to get drilled.

"I'm Jack Anderson, Edna's son-in-law, and you are?" Jack asked, staring warily into Christoff's unusual eyes.

Edna paused in pouring the shot of whiskey into her coffee cup and waited. An amused smile curved her lips when Christoff finally spoke. Leave it to an alien to make a great first impression on the family.

"I am Christoff Anatu, from the village near the Dragon Claw Mountains. I am Edna's true mate. I claimed her last night," Christoff replied with a pleased grin.

"Oh," Jack muttered. "Is that in Europe somewhere?"

Edna turned in time to see Christoff frown and shake his head. She waited, counting, for the other shoe to fall. She almost made it to seven when he finally responded.

"No, Valdier. I am not from your world," Christoff said. "I have only been on your planet since yesterday. I do not know this Europe."

"Mom!" Shelly screeched. "You slept with a guy that you just met?!"

"Yes," Christoff responded before Edna had a chance to open her mouth to explain.

Edna didn't say anything. She wondered how long it would take

Shelly to comprehend the part where Christoff said that he was an alien. Lifting the cup to her lips, she took a sip of the hot liquid, enjoying the slight kick to it. Something told her today was going to be a very, very long day.

"Mom, I don't think Grandma sleeping with the guy is going to be the problem," Crystal interrupted in a shaky voice.

"Why…? Oh!" Shelly started to say before her voice faded.

Spark had decided to make an appearance. Instead of being in the huge cat-form or a dog like Bo, the symbiot looked like one of the stuffed teddy bears that adorned her bed. Crystal had given her a new one each year for her birthday and she always decorated the bed with them.

"Edna," Jack muttered, staring at the large golden bear. "What is that?"

"That is Spark, an alien symbiot that belongs to Christoff," Edna said calmly as the whiskey started to spread through her. "Christoff is an alien dragon-shifter from a planet somewhere off in space. The same ones that took Abby."

"That took…. Jack," Shelly said hoarsely. "I don't feel so good."

Edna watched as her daughter's eyes rolled back in her head as she fainted. Jack caught Shelly and lifted her into his arms. He staggered at first before deciding the couch was the closest stop. Crystal scooted over, keeping a wary eye on Spark that was now sitting in front of her, returning her wide-eyed stare with a goofy grin on its face.

An hour later, they were all sitting around the dining room table. Edna and Christoff on one side and Jack and Shelly on the other. Crystal was sitting on the couch giggling at Spark. The symbiot was shifting into the animals that Crystal held up on her cell phone.

"Mom, watch this!" Crystal called out.

They all turned to watch as Spark turned into a unicorn with wings.

Crystal's delighted laughter filled the room when Spark leaned forward and brushed a long tongue up her cheek. Edna's eyes softened at the flushed face of her granddaughter.

"So, you arrived yesterday from another world, Christoff," Jack said with a strained smile. "It must have been a long trip."

"No," Christoff replied.

Jack swallowed and glanced at Edna. "Surely it must have taken years to get here? I believe I've read that it would take thousands of years just to journey to the next star system," he said.

"No," Christoff said again.

Edna finally took pity on her daughter and son-in-law. It was obvious from the possessive way Christoff was sitting next to her that he wasn't sure about them. Pulling her hand out of Christoff's, she looked at her daughter. Shelly was clenching her second cup of whiskey between her hands. She had asked for a cup of coffee and whiskey minus the coffee.

"Christoff doesn't remember how he got here," Edna replied. "It doesn't matter."

"How can you just accept an… an alien into your house like you've known him forever?" Shelly asked in a strained voice. "He gave you a hickey!"

"I gave her more than that," Christoff growled, tucking his hand back into Edna's again.

"Christoff," Edna chided. "You are not helping the situation."

"I know," Christoff replied with a grin.

Edna bit back a laugh at the mischievous gleam in his eyes. He was having fun. Her gaze swept over to where Crystal was laughing and running her hands over Spark. That alone was enough to bring tears to her eyes.

"Mom," Shelly groaned, dropping her head into her hands as she leaned against the table.

"I met another alien before," Edna finally admitted. "I came to pick up Bo and Gloria. Abby was watching them for me so I could drive down for Crystal's birthday. When I arrived, Abby wasn't alone anymore. A man with gold eyes was with her. He took me up to the high meadow."

"Why?" Jack asked.

Edna swallowed and squeezed Christoff's hand. "So that I could understand him. His symbiot was there, but it was much larger. It was in the shape of a space ship. When we stepped inside it, I could understand what Zoran was saying. He told me that he planned to take Abby back with him to his world." She reached out with her other hand and touched the small globe sitting in the middle of the table. "This proves he did."

"Is Christoff going to take you back to his world?" Shelly asked, fear lacing her voice.

Edna glanced at Christoff when he squeezed her hand. She had never thought of that. Would he return to his world, and if he did, would he expect her to go as well? A frown creased her brow.

"I do not know," Christoff replied, staring back at Shelly. "My symbiot is not large enough to be used as a transport, especially for intergalactic travel that would require a tremendous amount of energy."

"I don't think it is safe for him to remain here," Jack protested. "There is no way you could hide his… differences from everyone. Someone's bound to discover him."

Tears burned Edna's eyes at the thought of losing Christoff. Last night had been incredible. For the first time in years, she felt whole again.

"We'll take it one day at a time," she replied in a quiet voice. "We don't have to make a decision yet. It can wait until after Christmas."

CHAPTER ELEVEN

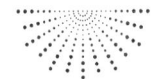

*C*hristoff watched as the young girl struggled to her feet. His gaze swept over the stiff material that made up her lower leg. She was quiet while she pulled on her high top boot, coat, scarf, and gloves. Bo danced around her with the tennis ball in his mouth, waiting to go out.

He rose from the chair where he had been watching Edna and Shelly decorate the tree with colorful lights and balls. Glancing at Spark, he motioned for the symbiot to follow Crystal and Bo. He nodded when he caught Edna's warm look of appreciation.

He grabbed his coat off the peg by the door and stepped outside, pulling the door closed behind him. Bo and Spark were running through the snow chasing each other and trying to snatch the green ball away. Crystal had walked over and sat down on the edge of the swing. Christoff walked over to stand next to her. For several long minutes, they just watched the two creatures play.

"What's it like where you come from?" Crystal suddenly asked in a soft voice.

Christoff glanced down at her for a moment, noting the haunted look in her eyes. He stepped closer to the swing and sat down beside her. He could feel the pain that was radiating out from her.

"It is very beautiful," he replied, picturing the valley and the mountains surrounding it. "Or it was."

"Was? What happened to it?" Crystal asked, turning to look at him in curiosity.

Christoff shrugged. "My mountain erupted. I am not sure how much damage was done. The first time it did, there was a lot of damage… and several of my people were killed, including my parents," he explained in a somber tone.

"What did you do?" Crystal asked.

"I went to the mountain to calm it," he said, looking out over the yard.

"Did you? Did you calm the mountain?" she asked.

"Yes," he murmured. "For several centuries until it would not sleep any longer."

Christoff heard Crystal's swift inhalation of air. He smiled at her when she stared at him in awe. He had never had anyone look at him like that before.

Well, except Edna last night, he thought with a grin.

"How? I mean, seriously? Centuries? Cool," she muttered.

"Yes," he replied in amusement. "It is very cold out."

"No, cool, that you could calm a mountain," she corrected, her voice dropping as it turned sad again.

"Why are you sad? I can smell your pain," Christoff asked in curiosity this time.

Crystal tucked her head in her jacket and turned her gaze down to the floor. A mutinous expression crossed her face and she held up her left leg. He frowned when she nodded at it.

"I shouldn't have lived," she whispered.

"Why do you believe that?" he asked.

"My friend Stacy was supposed to sit in the back seat with me, but we had gotten into a fight," she said with a sniff. "It was so stupid. I don't even remember why we were mad at each other."

"What happened?"

Crystal stared at her leg and wiped an angry tear away. He could see her struggling to compose herself and waited. He knew what her grief was like. He had felt the same way for many years after his parents' deaths. It was only as time passed and he grew older that he understood that life and death came without any guarantees.

"Stacy's mom lost control on an icy patch of road and went over the side of the highway. I remember the car rolling and rolling and rolling. I didn't think it was ever going to stop," Crystal said, her voice haunted by the memory. "Stacy wasn't wearing a seat belt and was thrown from the car. Her mom was pinned by the steering wheel. That whole front of the car was smashed in. I was in the back seat. My lower leg was crushed. When I woke up again, it was gone. Now… now, I'm just broken."

Christoff scowled. "Why do you call yourself broken? I do not see you as broken," he asked.

Crystal looked up at him. Angry tears glittered in her eyes as she stared defiantly at him. She pursed her lips and refused to answer.

"You think it is because you are different from the other younglings?" he asked, tilting his head to study her. "They have been mean to you?"

Crystal bowed her head, shaking it in denial. "No," she admitted. "It's just… I can't do the things the other kids can do."

"If your friend Stacy had lived and lost a part of her leg, would you think of her as broken?" he asked.

"Of course not," Crystal muttered. "She'd still be my best friend."

"You can walk. I have seen you. Other younglings can also do this, yes?" he pointed out.

"Yes, but not like I used to," she snapped, sitting up to glare at him. "I know what you are trying to do. Mom and the counselor I've been going to have tried the same thing."

"But, they do not understand what it feels like to not be whole," he added in a quiet voice, putting her feelings into words. "I do. I… was… am like you, not quite whole."

Crystal frowned and looked him over. "You don't look broken to me," she replied.

Christoff looked at where Bo and Spark were now sitting on the porch. He glanced at Crystal and grinned. Standing up, he held his hand out to her.

"Would you like to go for a sleigh ride?" he asked.

"A sleigh ride?" Crystal asked in confusion, looking around the yard. "Grandma doesn't have a sleigh."

Christoff winked. "She may not have one, but I do," he assured her. "Come, let us see if your mother and Edna would like to go for ride."

"What does this have to do with you and me being broken?" Crystal asked with a sardonic twist to her lips.

"Everything," he promised.

"Okay," Crystal replied with a shrug. "But this isn't going to work."

Christoff smiled down at Crystal, but didn't respond. Instead, he opened the door to the cabin and peeked inside. Edna looked up at him with a raised eyebrow.

"I would like to take you, Shelly, and Crystal for a sleigh ride," Christoff said formally.

Edna smiled in confusion. "But, I don't have a sleigh. All I have is the skid for hauling wood and Gloria can't pull all of us even if I did," she said, walking toward him.

"I have a sleigh," he promised. "I want to show Crystal that even those that are different are not necessarily broken."

"Oh!" Edna exclaimed, glancing at where Shelly was standing and listening. "Let's go for a sleigh ride."

"Crystal?" Shelly asked in a worried tone.

"It is time for her to heal," Christoff murmured. "Come."

Christoff stepped back and shut the door. He motioned for Crystal to follow him. She stopped on the middle step, her expression mutinous again.

With a wave of his hand, his symbiot swept down the steps around Crystal. It turned to liquid before reforming into a sleigh similar to what they used back on his world. He watched Crystal's mouth drop open before it snapped shut when he grinned at her.

"You still need a horse to pull it," she informed him with a raised eyebrow.

"Not a horse, but a dragon," he said, stepping back and shifting.

"Holy sh…!" Crystal started to say before clamping her mouth shut when the door behind her opened.

"What the fuck?" Shelly choked out in disbelief.

"Mom!" Crystal growled in disapproval at her mother's language, glancing over her shoulder.

Edna's laughter echoed through the yard. "Go," she said, waving her hand.

"But… What if Jack comes back while we're gone?" Shelly muttered, trying to push back into the house.

"Then, he'll wait for us," Edna said firmly, pushing her daughter between her shoulder blades. "It will take him hours to get to Shelby, find clothes to fit Christoff, and return. Come on."

Shelly glared at her mother. "Since when did you become so adventuresome?" she demanded, pulling her hat down over her ears and starting across the porch.

"Come on, Mom!" Crystal laughed, climbing into the sleigh. "It even made steps for me!"

"Awesome," Shelly replied weakly as she descended the steps and crossed the snow-covered path to the sleigh. "How is that… that thing supposed to pull this?"

Christoff turned his head and snorted at Shelly. Stepping in front of the sleigh, he growled out a command to his symbiot to create a harness for him. Within seconds, golden straps formed over Christoff's chest.

"It's not a thing, Mom, it's Christoff. He's a dragon, too," Crystal breathed.

"I… Why is the seat so warm?" Shelly asked nervously as she sat down. "It feels like this thing has a built-in heater."

Edna laughed again. "And a blanket, it would appear," she giggled when a thin blanket suddenly flowed over their laps. "Hang on. We're ready when you are, Christoff," she called out.

Christoff snorted again and took off. He might not be as big as the other dragons, but all the work on the mountain and climbing had built up his muscles. He wasn't tall, but he was thickly built and had a tremendous endurance.

He tossed his head and drew in a deep breath of frigid air, enjoying the feeling of being outside. He briefly glanced over his shoulder and fluttered his deformed wings before winking at Crystal. Her eyes grew round as she understood what he meant by being broken as well. A small, trembling smile pulled her lips upward and she nodded to him.

A feeling of warmth and happiness flooded him and he broke into a trot as he headed up the path to the upper meadow. The snow wasn't as deep on the path and he could have gone faster, but he was enjoying the slow, steady pace.

It be more fun with my mate, his dragon snorted, glancing back at where Edna was talking with Shelly.

In time, Christoff cautioned. *Last night was a first for both of us. I do not want to scare her away. We came close to losing her.*

Not no more, his dragon argued. *She ready. I call.*

No! Her family is just now accepting this, Christoff argued.

They accept my mate, too, his dragon snapped.

Christoff could feel his dragon straining to break free of his control. He couldn't blame him. After last night, he could feel the change in him. He felt the empty void that had been tearing him apart seal, making him whole for the first time in his life. His dragon wanted his mate as well.

Soon, Christoff promised.

Better, his dragon pouted. *I ready. I horny.*

Christoff laughed. *Just keep it hidden. I would hate to shock Shelly any more than we have, not to mention Crystal is too young to see a fully aroused male dragon.*

His dragon shrugged. *She close her eyes,* he suggested.

Christoff released a groan. His dragon was not going to make this easy – on either of them. He just hoped that he could keep control until after Edna's family left. If not, they might be getting an eyeful after all.

CHAPTER TWELVE

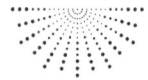

*I*t was late that night before Jack, Shelly, and Crystal left. Christoff stood on the porch with his arms wrapped around Edna. Jack had returned in time for dinner and had listened in bewildered amusement as Crystal told him about the sleigh ride. Afterwards, they had sat around the brightly lit tree. Shelly, Edna, and Crystal sang songs of bells and snowmen and other lively tunes while he and Jack sat listening and talking.

Christoff's eyes darkened to a deep gold as he remembered the other man's heartfelt thanks as he watched his daughter. He could feel the love the man had for her, and his pain. He remembered the look in his own father's eyes so long ago.

"She will be alright," Christoff murmured.

Jack sipped on the hot mug of chocolate that Shelly had handed him a few minutes before. Christoff had chosen the dark amber liquid that Edna had poured into her coffee earlier. Jack had turned it down, explaining that he would be driving and the roads would be hazardous enough without him adding alcohol to it.

"How do you know? Granted, she is like a different girl than the one that was here earlier, but

I worry," Jack said with a sigh.

"All parents do," Christoff replied. "I see the same look in your eyes that was in my father and mother's. I did not want to disappoint them. They believed in me when I did not believe in myself. Crystal will be the same. She will fight at first because she will not disappoint you, but in the end, it will be because she does not want to disappoint herself."

"I hope you're right," Jack said. "I really hope you are right."

Christoff smiled as he remembered the hug that Crystal had given him before she left. He hadn't known what to do at first. It was Edna's nod of encouragement that had him wrapping his arms awkwardly around the young girl.

"Thank you," she whispered.

Christoff leaned back and smiled. "We are given certain tasks in life. It is not the task, but the way we handle them that will guide who we are to become. You are strong and beautiful, just like your mother and grandmother. Never forget the power inside you."

"Did you ever forget?" Crystal asked softly.

Christoff knew he could lie, but he wouldn't. He stared into Crystal's anxious green eyes and nodded. Yes, he had forgotten for a time.

"We all forget at one time or another," he admitted ruefully.

"Let's go inside," Christoff murmured. "I don't want you getting cold."

Edna laughed and looked down at the sweater she was wearing. Normally, she would have a pair of thermals, several shirts, her thickest jacket, hat, gloves, scarves, and anything else she could think of to keep warm. Since last night, she felt like a different woman, one with a built-in heater that would make menopause look like a day in the sauna.

Christoff felt her pull away from him so she could see his face. He returned her gaze with a steady one of his own. He knew she wanted to know what happened last night.

Tell her, his dragon snorted. *Then I get my mate.*

"What happened last night?" Edna asked, confirming his fear. "Ever since we made love – ever since you bit me – I feel different."

"That is because you are," he murmured, looking out over the yard. "My dragon wants his mate."

"Your dragon – how?" Edna asked in confusion. "I mean, there aren't any girl dragons around and I'm not about to let you…."

Christoff shook his head. "My dragon wants his mate," he whispered, taking a step closer to her. "In here."

He watched as she followed his finger down to where it was pointing at her chest. A frown creased her brow. She looked back up at him and shook her head.

"I don't understand," she whispered.

"Do you trust me?" he asked in a husky voice.

She blinked several times before she scowled at him. "Of course I trust you," she said.

"Then, come to me," he growled in a deeper, rough tone. "Come to me, my mate."

Edna gasped when she felt a primitive reaction to his command. Her eyes widened when she heard a whisper echo in her head. She turned to look out at the yard. Everything seemed clearer, more vivid than before. Blinking, she looked down at her hands and saw them shimmering with a pale green light before she blinked again and she saw…

Claws? she squeaked.

Turning, she stumbled when she almost tripped over her tail. Freezing on the porch, she turned around again, slower this time. A hiccup escaped her when she saw her reflection in the window. She swallowed as she looked into the familiar, yet unfamiliar, green eyes staring back at her. The expression in them, she knew, it was the face that went with the eyes that she didn't.

Christoff, she whispered in terror.

I am here, he murmured.

She turned her head to stare at the ruby and silver dragon standing in the snow just off the porch. He was looking at her with an expression of hope and fear. She opened her mouth to lick her suddenly dry lips and discovered sharp teeth instead.

What am I? she asked, beginning to tremble.

You are beautiful. You are Edna. You are my true mate, he replied, taking a step closer to the porch. *Will you come to me?*

Edna blinked several times as the shock of what happened washed through her. She looked down at her body again, this time noting the delicate scales and the tiny ruby and silver pattern etched into them. She felt warm, but not unbearably.

It dragon fire, a soft, tentative voice whispered.

What?! Who? What is going on? Edna demanded, turning in a circle and knocking against the swing, causing it to rock wildly back and forth.

I your dragon, the voice replied. *My mate call to me. I go.*

What? Wait a minute. Your mate? Christoff said his dragon needed his mate. Can I change back? Edna asked desperately.

"Yes," Christoff said, stepping up onto the porch.

Edna turned her head, surprised to see Christoff in his two-legged form. She trembled when he reached out to tenderly stroke her jaw. A soft purr escaped her and her eyelashes closed for a moment at his touch.

"Think of yourself as Edna," he whispered.

Edna opened her eyes and stared back at Christoff. She started when she saw her hand lift to touch his chest. Staring at it, she turned it over. It was back to normal. Her head jerked up to stare at him.

"What happened?" she asked in a husky, slightly strained tone.

"It is the dragon fire," he admitted, touching her jaw with the tips of his fingers. "It can only be given to a true mate. You survived the gift from my dragon. He watched as his mate was born. She lives inside you now. But, just as I need you, he needs her. He is lonely."

And horny, his dragon interjected.

She watched Christoff wince. "And horny," he added with a grimace. "He insisted I tell you that."

"I wonder where he gets that from," she commented dryly.

Christoff shrugged. "I have centuries to make up for – and so does he," he muttered.

"Did he tell you that as well?" she asked with a raised eyebrow.

Christoff gave her that boyish grin that melted her heart. A soft chuckle escaped her. In just two days, he had totally wrapped her around his little finger. For a moment, Edna thought of the beauty of Christoff's ruby and silver dragon. A wave of heat flashed through her and she could feel *her* dragon shifting uncomfortably.

Let me guess. You're horny, too, aren't you? Edna asked with a sigh.

A soft snort sounded through her head. *He very cute,* her dragon admitted.

Alright, have fun, Edna replied. *Just don't do anything I wouldn't.*

Almost immediately, Edna released a groan. She probably shouldn't have said that, considering everything she and Christoff had done last night. In a flash, she felt the odd shifting again before the world righted itself. With a snort, she bounded off the porch and turned, waving her tail in the air. A moment later, the loud roar of the male sounded behind her as she ran up the path to the high meadow. She had almost made it when she felt the sting of his teeth as he sank them into her neck. A sudden wave of fire poured through her.

Not again, Edna groaned as the heat built and she felt her body burst into waves of feverish desire.

Yes, mine! Christoff's dragon roared, pulling her tail to the side so he could mount her from behind. *Yes!*

Fire exploded inside the small dragon as the male's long cock slid between the protective slit until it was embedded deep inside her. Her dragon shuddered with pleasure as her mate took her for the first time. Edna had to admit, it was having a profound effect on her as well.

The male continued to breathe his fire into her bloodstream, letting it spread through her until she was writhing under him. He kept his tail wrapped around hers so that she could not try to escape him. Positioning his larger frame over her, he held her captive beneath his body as he began to rock back and forth in a slow, possessive mating that sent bursts of pleasure coursing through her.

The female groaned when she felt her mate shift his weight. The move pushed him deeper into her, pulling a hoarse cry as he sought her womb. The rough, thick cock stroked her softer channel and she grew slick and hot. As the heat built, she tilted her hips up so that he could push even deeper. A series of low, rough grunts escaped them as they came together in a primitive mating that shook the ground.

Edna gasped when her dragon was suddenly released. The emptiness from where he had been impaled in her left her feeling off balance and desperate. That feeling was quickly swept away when he rolled her over onto her back and sank down until their bellies rubbed as he slid back into her. She snapped at him, desperate to ignite her own fire inside him. It took three tries before she was able to grab the soft underside of his neck.

Biting down, she breathed her own fire into him. A searing triumph soared through her when she heard his roar and his cock thickened and began to pulse inside her. Her own body reacted to the overwhelming heat and fisted him in a tight hold as she pulsed around him, pulling out both of their orgasms until he collapsed on top of her with a soft groan.

Mine, he growled, licking her jaw. *Mine.*

CHAPTER THIRTEEN

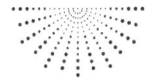

*E*dna rolled over beneath the covers and stared at Christoff's relaxed face. It had been almost a week since he came unexpectedly into her life and yet, it felt like forever. Lifting her hand, she touched his jaw.

"If you insist on touching me, I might have to sic my dragon on you," he murmured without opening his eyes.

"Not in the house," Edna admonished affectionately. "He almost caught his tail on fire last night," she reminded him.

Christoff's eyelashes slowly lifted and he smiled at her. She knew he was remembering their unexpected session on the rug in front of the fire. All the living room furniture ended up in the dining room. Poor Bo had finally given up on having any peace and gone into the guest bedroom.

"I need to get up and take Bo out and check on Gloria," Edna said with a sigh.

"I will do it," Christoff replied, rolling out of the bed. "You sleep in. It is your Christmas Eve, is it not?"

"Yes," Edna chuckled. "I need to get up. I'll take a shower while you take care of the animals."

Christoff's eyes darkened and he glanced at the bathroom. That was another place they had made love in. He had been thinking…

"No!" Edna interrupted his thought when she recognized the look that came into his eyes. She laughed and shook her head. "If you join me, I'll never get Christmas Eve dinner ready in time. We still need to move the furniture back as well."

She grinned at the scowl on Christoff's face. He hadn't been lying when he said he had a century's worth of lovemaking to catch up on. She just didn't know if she would survive it. She wouldn't have been able to move if not for his symbiot's skill in healing her soreness.

A gasp escaped her when his arms swept around her and he pressed a hot kiss to her shoulder. Damn, but he was incredibly sexy for an old man. The silver in his hair and the lines around his eyes and mouth just sent her body into overload.

He got good butt, too, her dragon whispered.

Shut up or we'll never get anything done. You, young lady, need to be grounded, Edna said as she pulled away with a look of warning.

Edna ignored the snort of her dragon as she stepped into the bathroom. She had a lot to do before Jack, Shelly, and Crystal came over this afternoon. Spending it in bed was not part of the well-ordered plan that she had written in her head.

She gave the image in the mirror a critical look as she released the braid in her long hair. Wiggling her nose, she decided that she looked and felt younger. Impulsively, her fingers lifted to touch the mark on her neck. If she wasn't careful, she would forget her resolve and say to hell with Christmas Eve dinner. She had some TV dinners in the freezer. Frozen turkey and dressing might be needed in an emergency.

Christoff patted Gloria as he entered her stall. He quickly set to work cleaning it and giving her fresh straw, water, and feed. It was supposed to snow again today, so she would have to stay inside where it was warmer. He was just hanging up the tools he used when he felt the strange sensation that he wasn't alone.

Danger? he asked his dragon, trying to sense where the feeling was coming from.

I no smell another. Only beast, his dragon replied.

Turning, he gazed around the small barn. Reaching out, he grabbed the pitchfork and held it tightly in his right hand. With a word of warning to his dragon, he walked along the three stalls. He had just peered into the last one when he felt the presence behind him and turned.

The pitchfork in his hand vanished and he stared in shock at the elegant, golden figure of a woman. She smiled serenely at him as she glided across the floor. He swallowed when she stopped a few feet from him and studied him in silence.

"You!" he choked out. "It was you. I remember now. You were in the cave – right before the mountain erupted. You spoke to me."

"Yes," Aikaterina murmured.

"Why?"

"The younglings," she whispered, looking around her. "They wished to give you the gift of Christmas. They were willing to risk their lives to give it to you."

"They gave me gifts," Christoff replied in a soft voice.

"They gave you love, friendship, and acceptance," Aikaterina agreed with a smile. "I wished to give you a gift of my own. I see that it was the right one, Old Dragon of the Mountain."

"Yes. Edna… She is my true mate," Christoff replied in a thick voice.

"She will be a good companion for you back on your world," Aikaterina said with a smile.

"But, I cannot leave," Christoff said with a frown. "Edna has a child and grandchild here. She will not want to leave them."

Aikaterina gazed at him with a sad smile and shook her head. "You cannot stay on this world, Christoff. It is not safe for you, your dragon, or your symbiot. They will die if you try to stay here and so will you," she whispered sadly. "I can give you until midnight tomorrow night, but then I must return you and your mate to Valdier."

"No," Christoff protested, watching as the Goddess started to fade. "Please."

"Midnight Christmas, Old Dragon, then you must return," her voice echoed.

Christoff stood in the middle of the barn, his eyes burning with anger and defeat. He knew there was no way he could fight her. Clenching his fists, he stared down at the ground until he felt a measure of calm. He would tell Edna tonight after her family left. She would have one more day with them before she would have to say goodbye to them forever. He just hoped that she didn't hate him for it.

"Are you alright?" Edna asked for the hundredth time that day.

Christoff looked up from where he was placing the cookies on the round tray. They had moved the furniture back into place and finished wrapping the last of the presents that Edna had hidden throughout the year. She had laughed and shared stories of Christmases past with him throughout the day. Now, they were waiting for Jack, Shelly, and Crystal to arrive.

"I'm fine," he said with a smile. "This is a lot of food."

"Part of the tradition is eating leftovers for a week, so you don't want any more for another year," Edna laughed as she pulled yet another dish out of the oven.

Christoff's head turned and he listened. "They are here," he said, popping the last cookie that wouldn't fit onto the platter into his mouth.

"You aren't going to eat any dinner if you keep doing that," Edna teased as she hurried to the door. "Come on, Bo. Come on, Spark. Go welcome them."

Christoff watched as Edna hurried to the door. Love and fear battled inside him. A part of him wanted to roar at the Goddess for her interference. How dare she give him his every hope and desire, only to threaten it now? He pushed the feeling away. He would not dampen the time Edna had left with her child. As he had told Crystal, life came with no guarantees. He would do everything he could to make Edna happy back on his world. He only hoped that she would give him and his world a chance.

"Grandma, this one is for you," Crystal said a couple of hours later.

The house had been filled with laughter as Shelly, Jack, and Crystal brought in colorful wrapped gifts to go under the tree. Shortly after that, they had eaten. Eventually, the kitchen was cleaned and everyone was groaning about having eaten too much.

The festivities moved back into the living room so everyone could stretch out in comfort. Now, they were doing a Christmas Eve exchange as Jack and Shelly would be going to a party tomorrow with friends of theirs.

"This one is for you, Christoff," the young girl added with a smile.

Christoff looked up in surprise. He had nothing for any of the others. Reaching out, he took the red and green box from her.

"I have nothing for you," he replied quietly, feeling bad.

Crystal shook her head. "I was thinking about what you said the other day. Mom and I talked as well. I'm going to start school in January and see how it goes. Baby steps. I want to see my friends again and maybe, hopefully, make new ones," she whispered, glancing at where her parents and grandmother were talking and laughing. "I've got something else for you, as well."

Christoff frowned when Crystal stood up and waved for him to follow her. His gaze swept to Edna for a moment. She was looking back at him while listening to Jack.

"Come on," Crystal urged in excitement. "Spark, I need you to come with us, too."

His symbiot shimmered with color and rose up. Christoff could feel its excitement. He stepped over to the door and helped Crystal with her coat before grabbing his own off the peg. A moment later, they were outside in the yard.

The sky was a brilliant blue and the sun shone down. It was still too cold for the snow to melt, but it was the perfect day for being outside. He would need to let Gloria out for a while. His dragon could clear the snow and dry the ground in just a few minutes.

"What is it you wish to show me?" Christoff asked, watching in amusement as his symbiot pressed against the little girl and nodded at something she was showing it.

Crystal limped over to him. Holding out the paper in her hand, she motioned for Christoff to take it. He carefully pulled the heavy paper toward him. Blinking in surprise, he saw that it was a picture of a dragon. It didn't take long to see that it was a picture of him, only….

"The wings," he murmured, touching the gold colored wings on his dragon's back.

Crystal smiled. "I thought about it over the last few days. If they could make me a fake leg that worked, why couldn't we make you wings? Spark can change into anything. You said he was smaller than the other ones of his kind, but he is plenty big enough to make you a set of wings to fit over yours. I… Do the dragons in your world fly?" she asked in a tentative voice.

Christoff fingered the drawing. "Yes, they fly but I have never been able to," he murmured, looking back at her with burning eyes. "This is what you were doing earlier. I saw you with my symbiot."

Crystal nodded shyly. "I was showing him how my leg worked," she replied in a soft voice. "I thought it was worth a try."

Christoff suddenly laughed. "Yes, it is worth a try. I honestly never thought of it before," he admitted, handing her back the drawing. Turning to look at his symbiot, he grinned. "Are you willing to try it, my friend?"

Familiar warmth filled him as it responded. Focusing, he called eagerly to his dragon. Within seconds, he had shifted. Crystal's delighted giggle told him that she enjoyed watching him in his dragon form.

"I really hope this works," Crystal clapped in excitement. "I'd love to see a dragon fly."

CHAPTER FOURTEEN

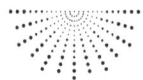

*C*hristoff heard Crystal's heartfelt wish. Something deep down inside told him that this was very important not just for him, but for her as well. She needed to know that one day she could fly as well and that her leg would not hold her back from achieving her dreams.

A shiver ran through Christoff's dragon when he felt the symbiot form wings over his small, deformed ones. His dragon shook, not used to the unfamiliar weight on his back. Focusing, Christoff sucked in a breath when he felt the wings spread out. He turned his head to stare at the golden extensions to his body.

He spent several minutes experimenting with the weight, feel, and movement of them. His dragon was impatient to lift off, but Christoff understood the overall importance of this being successful.

We need to make sure this will work, Christoff explained to his impatient dragon. *This is about more than us, it is also about Crystal.*

I know. I ready, his dragon insisted. *Spark ready. We work as one. It is way we are made.*

If you are sure….

Christoff never got to finish his thought. The moment his dragon felt him concede, he pushed up off the ground. The instinctive knowledge of how to fly filled the creature. It was the same as the knowledge of how to breathe dragon fire and shift from one form to the other without thought that had been passed down through generation after generation of dragons. A wave of awe washed through him as he lifted off the ground. His golden wings moved in powerful strokes up and down, pushing him higher.

"Go, Christoff! Go!" Crystal yelled, laughing and trying to follow him. "Fly to the moon and back!"

The dragon released a low rumble of laughter that echoed through the crisp mountain air. For the first time in his life, he was flying! Really flying!

I free, his dragon whispered to him in awe. *I like other dragons now. I not weak, unworthy.*

You have never been weak or unworthy, my friend. You have always been perfect to me, he replied in a somber voice.

I wish my mate to see me, his dragon sighed.

She does, Christoff chuckled. *Look to your right side.*

Christoff felt his dragon's love for its mate explode through him. He knew what it was feeling. He felt the same way whenever he looked at Edna. Slowing his speed to match his mate, the large male waited for the small green female to catch up with him. Together, they flew over the trees and up to the high meadow. Christoff circled around before gliding in for a landing along the powdered snow. He turned as his mate came in behind him, her soft rumble of happiness washing over him as he folded his make-shift wings against his side.

You fly, his mate breathed out in wonder.

Yes, I fly, he laughed. *I fly!*

Crystal turned to look at her parents. Tears burned her eyes, but she quickly blinked them back. It was true. If Christoff could fly, so could she. Walking slowly toward her parents, she didn't think about the slight limp caused by her prosthetic. It was her symbiot. Her way of being able to fly.

"It worked," she said with a smile. "Just like with me, his wings worked."

"Yes," Shelly whispered, brushing at the tears streaming down her cheeks. "Oh, Crystal."

Crystal moved up the steps and into her mom and dad's arms. She buried her face against her mom and sobbed. It took several minutes to finally calm herself enough to realize that they were all getting cold.

"I'm going to be okay now," she said, wiping at the tears on her face. "I know I can fly, just like Christoff."

"Yes, you can," her dad murmured. "You always could."

Crystal gave her dad a shaky laugh. "That's pretty much what Christoff told me. Isn't it cool that Grandma is a dragon?" she added with a grin.

Shelly looked up into the sky and shook her head in wonder. Her mom! A dragon. How cool would that have been during some of the mother-daughter events when she was growing up, she thought in disbelief before a wave of sadness washed through her. Her mom had told her that she would be leaving soon, that she and Christoff couldn't stay here.

"A woman came to me," her mom had told them while they were inside after Christoff and Crystal went outside.

"A woman? What kind of woman?" Shelly asked, puzzled.

Edna looked down at her hands. She grasped them together when she saw they were shaking. A single tear ran down her cheek and dropped on it, but she knew what she had to do. In life, a child could accept that their parents would go first. It was time for Edna to go, but not in the way most parents do.

"She was like Spark, only more powerful, I suspect. She explained that she sent Christoff here, but that he could not stay. It is too dangerous for him… and for me, now," Edna explained. "I belong with him, Shelly. I love him so much. I love you and Jack and Crystal, but this is different. It is more than about me. He is a good man."

"I know he is, Mom, but why do you have to leave?" Shelly insisted, rising from her chair and pacing.

"Shelly," Jack murmured, standing as well and holding her. "He's an alien. It would only be a matter of time before someone discovered him. You know what would happen to him, and your mom, if they did. We talked about this over the last few days."

"I know, but why does she have to leave?" she insisted. "I need you!"

"No, you don't," Edna replied, standing. "And that is the way it is supposed to be. You have Jack and Crystal. You'll always have me inside your heart. I won't be truly gone as long as you remember that, just as your dad has never been gone for me. I can feel him in my heart. Just because I can't see or touch him anymore doesn't mean he isn't there. I need to be with Christoff, Shelly. He makes me feel young and alive. He fills the emptiness left by your dad."

"You love him, don't you?" Shelly asked in a husky voice.

"Yes, very much," Edna replied, walking around to hold her daughter's hands. "Just as you love Jack and I loved your father."

They all turned to look when they heard Crystal shouting out in the front yard. Striding to the door, they quickly grabbed their coats and slid them on before stepping outside. Edna was the first down the steps. She could feel her mate's excitement and joy. Staring up at the beautiful sight of the male dragon in flight, she called to her own dragon.

Can we join him? she breathed out, staring in awe as the male flew higher.

Yes, her dragon whispered as she took over.

In the background, Edna heard Crystal's excited laugh that she had the coolest grandmother ever at the same time as she heard Shelly's gasp of disbelief. She ignored them all, focusing instead on her mate.

Lifting off the ground, she felt an intense wave of joy and happiness fill her as she raced to catch up with him. Her gaze ran over the golden wings encasing his shorter ones. The membrane of them was so sheer that she could see through them. His warm rumble of pleasure washed over her and she angled her small body up beside him.

My mate, she breathed.

Christoff turned and slowed so she could catch up with him. Together, they soared over the tops of the snow-covered trees and up the mountain. From this height, Edna could see for miles. Now, she truly understood what the golden woman was saying. This is what her and Christoff's dragons needed. Shelly and Crystal would be alright. It was time for her to move on to her next life.

CHAPTER FIFTEEN

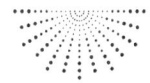

*C*hristmas morning came bright and early. Jack, Shelly, and Crystal had decided to stay the night. They had stayed up late, laughing, talking, and singing. Spark had made a bed for Crystal and she and Bo were still curled up in the golden symbiot's warm embrace when the adults rose.

"I remember you waking us up at the crack of dawn so you could open your presents," Edna reflected in a soft voice as she moved around the kitchen.

"Crystal used to do that, but she stopped after the accident," Shelly replied, pulling the milk, orange juice, and eggs out of the refrigerator. "Pancakes and eggs?"

"Sounds great," Edna said. "I think she'll be alright now."

"Yes," Shelly replied, glancing into the living room. "She wants to start back to regular school after the first of the year."

Edna glanced at her daughter's worried face. "Let her, Shelly. She knows what she needs to heal," she advised in a soft tone.

Shelly smiled and nodded. "When do you leave?" she asked in a trembling voice.

"I think tonight," Edna replied, turning Shelly in her arms and staring into her eyes. "We will not be sad. There may be a way to come back. If there is, I'll find it. I don't want this to be a sad day."

"I know," Shelly whispered. "What about the cabin? All of your things?"

"I drew up a will shortly after your father died. I revised it when Abby left me this. The cabin and mountain will go to Crystal. Abby would be happy with that. I contacted a lawyer in Wyoming to handle things," Edna replied. "I know Jack could have, but I didn't want anything suspicious coming back on you two with my leaving. Chad Morrison knows about the aliens. He is managing Paul Grove's ranch. From what he told me, the aliens have a tendency to show up when he least expects it. Paul left his ranch as a place where they could arrive without fear of being discovered."

"When did you do this?" Shelly asked in surprise.

Edna smiled. "When you have an alien goddess appear before you, you tend to realize that anything is possible when you set your mind to it. I called Chad immediately and made the arrangements," she replied dryly.

Shelly shook her head in amazement. "I love you, Mom. I'm happy for you, too. You have been the best mom any girl could wish for," she said in a thick voice.

Edna wrapped her arms around her daughter and held her tight. "You do the same for Crystal and I know that my work is done," she whispered. "I love you, too, Shelly, never forget that. I'm proud of you, too. You are a wonderful mother, daughter, and wife."

"Hey, the mule is fed, is there any food for the men?" Jack called out as he stomped his feet by the door to knock the snow off of them. He winced when both women hissed at him to be quiet. "Sorry!"

"I'm hungry, too," Crystal groaned out in a sleepy voice. "Are we having pancakes?"

Later that afternoon, Edna and Christoff stood on the porch watching as Jack, Shelly, Crystal, Bo, and Gloria headed back down the mountain. Christoff had looked at her funny when she told him that Bo and Gloria would be going to live with Jack, Shelly, and Crystal.

She had hugged the Golden before piling all of his toys, food, and bedding into the back of the SUV. He had helped Jack hitch the trailer and load Gloria. Edna had held out an apple for the old mule and stroked its head affectionately before pressing a kiss to its forehead.

"You know," he murmured, staring at the fading lights.

"Yes," she replied, turning to walk back into the house.

Christoff followed her inside and closed the door. The house seemed empty with everyone gone. Spark looked up at him, then at the door. He could see the small green tennis ball at its feet. He nudged the ball and watched as it rolled across the floor before looking at the door again.

"How?" he asked in a thick voice.

Edna smiled as she began picking up some of the dirty dishes that had been left out. Glancing over her shoulder, he could see the glimmer of amusement and acceptance in her eyes. She knew he was worried about her.

"An alien goddess told me," she said.

Christoff released the breath he was holding. He stared around the room. The warmth from the pellet stove and the fire kept the chill out. The colorful lights on the tree brightened the room and he could still smell the sweet scent of the pancakes they'd had for breakfast in the air. He would miss this. He had nothing to offer her when they returned to his world.

"Christoff," Edna murmured, setting the plates and glasses down on the counter and walking over to him. "It will be alright."

Christoff gazed down at Edna and pulled her into his arms. He held her tight against his body, savoring the feel of her soft form pressed against his. Lowering his head, he rested his chin against her hair.

"I love you, Edna," he murmured.

Edna's arms wrapped around his waist and she held him tightly against her. "I love you, too, my alien warrior," she whispered, relaxing.

They spent the rest of the day cleaning the cabin and organizing it. Edna had debated whether she should take the Christmas tree down or not and pack it away. Christoff made the decision when she told him that her family had always left it up until after the first of the year for good luck. They turned off the pellet stove and doused the fire in the fireplace before they went to bed.

Christoff watched as Edna brushed out her hair before she braided it. For a moment, she paused as she looked down at the bed. A look of confusion settled over her face.

"What's wrong?" he asked, walking over to tilt her face up so he could look into her eyes.

Edna gave a self-conscious laugh. "I don't know what to wear. Do we go to sleep in our clothes? Do I wear my nightgown? How is all this supposed to happen?" she asked nervously.

A smile curved Christoff's lips. "I plan to make love to you, so you won't be needing your clothes for a while. After that, it will be up to the goddess. Perhaps, she will let us know before we leave," he teased.

Edna raised her eyebrow. "If I appear on your world naked, I'm not going to be very happy with you," she warned.

"I'll take my chances," Christoff murmured before he bent and captured her lips.

Christoff glanced at the clock next to the bed. It was close to midnight. Edna lay tucked in his arms, sound asleep. They had made love, talked, and made love again. He knew she was frightened, but she never complained or expressed any doubt that she should return to his world with him. Exhaustion pulled at him as well. He worried that he wouldn't be able to care for her properly once he returned home. He would need to build them a home near the village. He debated if he should move to a different area, but something was pulling him back to the valley. It was as if something was telling him that this time, things would be different and he needed to go home.

His eyes drooped and no matter how hard he tried to keep them open, they refused. A strange warmth filled him as he fell into a deep slumber. He was vaguely aware that his symbiot had jumped onto the bed with them, but even that wasn't enough to pull him back to consciousness.

"Sleep, my gentle warrior. It is time for you and your mate to return home," Aikaterina whispered, stroking his brow. "You needn't worry. The villagers realize their mistake."

Christoff's lips moved, but no sound escaped. He finally gave up and slipped into the calm darkness, his arms tightening around Edna when he felt a sense of weightlessness. Home… Home.

EPILOGUE

*S*ix months later: Valdier

Edna laughed in delight as she watched Zohar reach for another cookie when he thought Abby wasn't looking. Abby, Zohar, and Zoran, the King of the Valdier, had been regular visitors since their arrival. Abby and Zoran had been visiting with the villagers and making sure that they had all the support they needed in the rebuilding of the village when she had seen Edna. Abby's cry of delight had drawn Edna's attention and before she knew it, she had been engulfed in her young friend's embrace.

"How...? Why...? I don't care," Abby had laughingly said as she brushed the tears from her cheeks.

"Edna, welcome to Valdier," Zoran had greeted, giving Christoff a puzzled look.

"I'm so glad you are here," Abby murmured, smiling as she reached out and moved the plate of cookies a little further away from the edge, and the greedy fingers trying to steal even more. "I know Shelly, Jack, and Crystal must miss you."

Edna blinked back the tears when she thought of her family back on Earth. She was discovering it was harder than she expected to leave them behind. Drawing in a deep breath, she gave Abby a weak smile.

"I promised myself I wouldn't dwell on what I can't change. My life is with Christoff now," Edna replied in a soft voice.

Abby bit her lip and bent to pick up Zohar when he peered over the side of the table. He had shifted into his dragon form in the hopes that he would be tall enough to reach the platter. Abby chuckled when he gave her a pitiful look.

"One more," she said in a stern voice. "Otherwise, you won't eat your dinner tonight."

"Cookie," Zohar grinned, shifting again and clapping his hands.

"I could talk to Zoran, Edna. They have ships that travel back and forth to Earth frequently now. Maybe they would be willing to come here," Abby suggested.

Edna's eyes lit up. She had never really thought of it as a possibility. Deep down, she had been afraid to ask Abby for fear of her saying that it was impossible.

"Oh, Abby, yes, please. I miss Shelly, Crystal, and Jack so much. If there is a chance for them to come here, life would be perfect," Edna replied with tears in her eyes.

Abby laughed. "I'll let Zoran know. He never says no to me," she retorted with a twinkle in her eye. "If he does, I have ways of making him change his mind," she added with a slight blush.

Edna laughed and reached over to squeeze Abby's hand. "I know exactly how you do it, too," she said with a wink. "It works with Christoff, as well."

Abby grinned and stood with a sigh. Zohar was getting sleepy and they needed to return to the palace. Holding her sleepy son in her arms, she watched as Edna stood up and wrapped her arms around Abby and Zohar.

"Thank you, Abby," Edna whispered in a husky voice. "Thank you for being such a wonderful friend."

Stepping back, they both turned when Zoran and Christoff came inside. A few minutes later, they watched as the trio took off, heading back over the mountains toward the ocean. She released a sigh of contentment and leaned against Christoff, their arms wrapped around each other.

"She's going to see if Zoran will bring Shelly, Jack, and Crystal to Valdier," Edna whispered.

"I know," Christoff replied, turning her toward him so he could gaze down at her with a small smile. "I asked Zoran if he would and he said yes. It should not be too long, there is already a ship headed toward Earth."

Edna shook her head and chuckled. "I should have known you were up to something when you asked Zoran to step outside to look at the new barn you are working on. Thank you," she said, her expression softening with love.

Christoff reached up and brushed a strand of silver hair back from her face. His expression was serious as he looked down at her. Tilting her chin, he paused a breath away from her lips.

"You never have to thank me for trying to make you happy, Edna. You are a treasure to me. I will do everything I can to make your life here good," he promised before capturing her lips.

Later that afternoon, Christoff released a groan when he heard his name being called. For half a second, he considered acting like he hadn't heard his brother. He wanted to retreat into the cottage where he would bar the doors in the hopes Lemar would get the message that he didn't want to deal with him. He would have if he thought it would work. Unfortunately, Edna would just make him unlock it.

"Christoff!" Lemar called out in greeting again when he didn't immediately answer.

Releasing a sigh of resignation, he slowly turned and scowled. His older brother was really beginning to become a pain in his backside. Ever since their return, Lemar had been trying to make up for all the centuries of rift between them. He hoped it didn't take that long for his brother to finally understand that he honestly didn't care. There was no changing the past and life was too full, and he was too happy, to care to dredge up hurt and hatred. Besides, he didn't think his parents would want him to.

He had to admit that Lemar had changed from the selfish, immature boy that he remembered. So had many of the villagers. The new village was still in the process of being built in the valley over from where the mountain had erupted. It would take time, but his skills and understanding of the rock foundations along with the history of it were helping to know where it was best to build their new homes and where to plant the crops needed to support the needs of the village.

"Lemar," Christoff replied bluntly.

"Be nice," Edna murmured, stepping out of the cottage he had built. "Hello, Lemar."

"Greetings, Edna," Lemar said with a grin. "I've found some new rocks. I wanted you to look at them."

Christoff shot Edna a pained glance before he grunted and held his hand out. Lemar dropped a pile of ugly rocks into his palm. Holding one of them up, he looked at it with a critical eye.

"Diamonds, they will work well for cutting," he grunted.

"Excellent," Lemar replied with a grin. "My mate wanted to know if you would honor us by coming to dinner tonight."

"No," Christoff started to reply before he grunted when Edna elbowed him.

"We would be delighted. I know the children are wanting to show Christoff their new rock collection and they wanted to see how his wings work," Edna interjected.

"I know," Lemar replied with a pleading look. "As you know, my youngest son, Anson, was injured during the eruption. One of his wings was crushed. His symbiot tried to heal it, but the damage was too great. By the time I found him, it could not be fixed and part of it had to be removed. Anson and his dragon have been very depressed since that happened. I would be forever in your debt if you would talk with him, Christoff. He will not listen to his mother or me. I… I understand now, just how grievous I was to you as a boy. I will understand if you say no, but please, I beg you to not blame my son for his father's behavior."

Christoff released a breath of resignation and ran his hand over his nape. He and Edna had been inundated by the older villagers that had been mean to him when he was young. The women cast looks of envy at Edna while the men tried to earn his forgiveness by helping him or bringing him tools. All he really wanted was for them to leave him alone.

"I will talk with Anson," he muttered, shooting Edna a look that promised he would take his revenge on her later. The slight, knowing smile on her lips showed him that she wasn't in the least bit intimidated by his threatening glare. "I will show him how he can use his symbiot to help him."

"I can talk with him as well," Edna said with a smile. "I wish my granddaughter, Crystal, was here. She would know what to say."

"Thank you," Lemar whispered in gratitude. "Thank you."

"I have work to do. Can you leave now?" Christoff asked in a blunt tone, grimacing when Edna snorted.

"Yes, yes, we will see you later this evening," Lemar replied, backing up and turning. "Until this evening, brother!"

Christoff watched as his older brother hurried down the path. Shaking his head, he glanced down at Edna when she wrapped her arm around his waist. A reluctant smile curved his lips when he saw her pleased expression.

"You know, we'll never be able to get rid of him now," he reflected accusingly.

"I know," she laughed. "He really isn't so bad."

"He is annoying," Christoff grumbled, turning her in his arms and pressing a kiss to her lips. "I have a present for you. I didn't get a chance to give you one on Christmas."

Edna raised an eyebrow and smiled up at him. "I think you gave me a beautiful Christmas gift," she teased. "If I remember correctly, I was pleasantly exhausted."

"This one is different," he said, reaching for her hand and lifting it so he could slide a ring onto it. "I saw the rings on your daughter and Jack's fingers. I asked them about it. They said it is a symbol of their commitment to each other. I wanted to give you a ring to show my love and commitment to you, Edna. I will never forget what you have given up to be with me here."

Edna stared at the ring he was slipping on her finger. It was big. It was made of gold with diamonds wrapping around it in a simple, yet elegant arrangement. She tilted her head when he gently touched her chin.

"I love you, my mate, forever," Christoff whispered. "Merry Christmas."

"Oh, Christoff," Edna murmured, reaching up to press a light kiss against his lips. "Didn't you know? You are my present. The only one I will ever need. I love you, my mate."

Neither one of them noticed the pale gold figure standing in the doorway of their cottage staring at them. Her expression was pleased, yet curious. Her fingers moved to the twin dragon necklaces around her neck. They had fallen off of Christoff in the cave. She had discovered them when she returned to make sure he had his satchel. Deciding that she would keep them as a gift to herself, she wondered what it would be like... to just once hold someone in her arms like Christoff was holding Edna.

Shaking her head at her fanciful thoughts, Aikaterina released a sigh and faded. She needed to check on the Hive. There was no telling what Arosa and Arilla had been up to in her absence. They were almost as bad as Amber and Jade, she thought as she opened the doorway back to her home.

Check out a video message from the Author!
https://www.youtube.com/watch?v=ZZbIjwGd0hI

Love this series? The next book is:
Pearl's Dragon
USA Today Bestseller!

Pearl St. Claire is enjoying a new adventure – learning to live on an alien planet. As a mature woman in her sixties, she thought she had experienced just about everything life could throw at her – only to discover she hasn't really experienced anything yet! She is both amused and exasperated when one of the dragon-shifting aliens kidnaps her, believing she is his true mate.

Life is no longer boring or lonely as Asim courts the enchanting and spirited human woman, especially when poachers attack, determined to steal the exotic creatures under his protection – including Pearl and a new clutch of alien eggs from Earth.

Check out the full book here: books2read.com/Pearls-Dragon

And if you'd love more dragonling adventures,

Night of the Demented Symbiots is for you!

As the night of the Halloween festival draws closer, the dragonlings, Roam, and Alice discover that the Queen of the Demented Symbiots plans to send her minions to capture the newest babies and take them to the land of Halloween! With their parents busy organizing the huge festival, the dragonlings and their friends are left with no choice but to prepare for the ultimate battle.

Check out the full book here:
books2read.com/night-of-the-demented-symbiots

Or read on for a sneak peek into a new series!

Touch of Frost
Magic, New Mexico Book 1
Sci-fi Romance and Paranormal Fantasy collide!

When a maximum-security fugitive escapes to a distant, forbidden planet whose inhabitants have not mastered space travel yet, it's Star Ranger Frost who is sent after him.

Lacey Adams is a widow who owns an animal shelter in Magic, New Mexico, an *unusual* small town, to say the least, and she is certainly not easily taken hostage, not by the fugitive and not by the Star Ranger who wants her for himself.

Check out the full book here: books2read.com/Touch-of-Frost

ADDITIONAL BOOKS

If you loved this story by me (S.E. Smith) please leave a review! You can discover additional books at: http://sesmithfl.com and http://sesmithya.com or find your favorite way to keep in touch here: https://sesmithfl.com/contact-me/ Be sure to sign up for my newsletter to hear about new releases!

Recommended Reading Order Lists:

http://sesmithfl.com/reading-list-by-events/

http://sesmithfl.com/reading-list-by-series/

The Series

Science Fiction / Romance

Dragon Lords of Valdier Series

It all started with a king who crashed on Earth, desperately hurt. He inadvertently discovered a species that would save his own.

Curizan Warrior Series

The Curizans have a secret, kept even from their closest allies, but even they are not immune to the draw of a little known species from an isolated planet called Earth.

Marastin Dow Warriors Series

The Marastin Dow are reviled and feared for their ruthlessness, but not all want to live a life of murder. Some wait for just the right time to escape….

Sarafin Warriors Series

A hilariously ridiculous human family who happen to be quite formidable… and a secret hidden on Earth. The origin of the Sarafin species is more than it seems. Those cat-shifting aliens won't know what hit them!

Dragonlings of Valdier Novellas

The Valdier, Sarafin, and Curizan Lords had children who just cannot stop getting into trouble! There is nothing as cute or funny as magical, shapeshifting kids, and nothing as heartwarming as family.

Cosmos' Gateway Series

Cosmos created a portal between his lab and the warriors of Prime. Discover new worlds, new species, and outrageous adventures as secrets are unravelled and bridges are crossed.

The Alliance Series

When Earth received its first visitors from space, the planet was thrown into a panicked chaos. The Trivators came to bring Earth into the Alliance of Star Systems, but now they must take control to prevent the humans from destroying themselves. No one was prepared for how the humans will affect the Trivators, though, starting with a family of three sisters….

Lords of Kassis Series

It began with a random abduction and a stowaway, and yet, somehow, the Kassisans knew the humans were coming long before now. The fate of more than one world hangs in the balance, and time is not always linear….

Zion Warriors Series

Time travel, epic heroics, and love beyond measure. Sci-fi adventures with heart and soul, laughter, and awe-inspiring discovery…

Paranormal / Fantasy / Romance

Magic, New Mexico Series

Within New Mexico is a small town named Magic, an… underlined unusual town, to say the least. With no beginning and no end, spanning genres, authors, and universes, hilarity and drama combine to keep you on the edge of your seat!

Spirit Pass Series

There is a physical connection between two times. Follow the stories of those who travel back and forth. These westerns are as wild as they come!

Second Chance Series

Stand-alone worlds featuring a woman who remembers her own death. Fiery and mysterious, these books will steal your heart.

More Than Human Series

Long ago there was a war on Earth between shifters and humans. Humans lost, and today they know they will become extinct if something is not done….

The Fairy Tale Series

A twist on your favorite fairy tales!

A Seven Kingdoms Tale

Long ago, a strange entity came to the Seven Kingdoms to conquer and feed on their life force. It found a host, and she battled it within her body for centuries while destruction and devastation surrounded her. Our story begins when the end is near, and a portal is opened….

Epic Science Fiction / Action Adventure

Project Gliese 581G Series

An international team leave Earth to investigate a mysterious object in our solar system that was clearly made by someone, someone who isn't from Earth. Discover new worlds and conflicts in a sci-fi adventure sure to become your favorite!

New Adult / Young Adult

Breaking Free Series

A journey that will challenge everything she has ever believed about herself as danger reveals itself in sudden, heart-stopping moments.

The Dust Series

Fragments of a comet hit Earth, and Dust wakes to discover the world as he knew it is gone. It isn't the only thing that has changed, though, so has Dust…

ABOUT THE AUTHOR

S.E. Smith is an *internationally acclaimed, New York Times* **and** *USA TODAY Bestselling* author of science fiction, romance, fantasy, paranormal, and contemporary works for adults, young adults, and children. She enjoys writing a wide variety of genres that pull her readers into worlds that take them away.

www.ingramcontent.com/pod-product-compliance
Lightning Source LLC
Chambersburg PA
CBHW070601180626
46817CB00005B/1945